RELIEF | A QUARTERLY CHRISTIAN EXPRESSION

VOLUME TWO | ISSUE THREE

RELIEF | A QUARTERLY CHRISTIAN EXPRESSION

EDITOR-IN-CHIEF
Kimberly Culbertson

ASSISTANT EDITORS
Heather von Doehren
Lisa Ohlen Harris

FICTION EDITOR
Alan Ackmann

CREATIVE NONFICTION EDITORS
Lisa Ohlen Harris
Jill Noel Kandel

POETRY EDITOR
Brad Fruhauff

TECHNICAL EDITOR
Coach Culbertson

EDITORIAL ASSISTANT
Margaret Krueger

GENRE READERS
Deanna Hershiser (CNF)
Linda MacKillop (CNF)

PROOFREADERS
Kristina Roth George
Kerr Bacchus
Amanda C. Bauch
Lindsay Crandall
Lee Ann Pingel

ADVISORS
Mick Silva
J. Mark Bertrand
Karen Miedrich-Luo

Relief: A Quarterly Christian Expression is published quarterly by ccPublishing, NFP, a 501(c)3 organization dedicated to advancing Christian literary writing. Mail can be sent to 60 W. Terra Cotta, Suite B, Unit 156, Crystal Lake, IL 60014-3548. Submissions are not accepted by mail.

SUBSCRIPTIONS

Subscriptions are $48 per year and can be purchased directly from the publisher by visiting http://www.reliefjournal.com. Single issues are also available.

COPYRIGHT

All works Copyright 2008 by the individual author credited. Anything not credited is Copyright 2008 by ccPublishing, NFP. No part of this publication may be reproduced, stored in a retrieval system, or transmitted by any means without prior written permission of ccPublishing, NFP.

SUBMISSIONS

Submissions are open year round via our Online Submisson System. Please visit our website at **http://www.reliefjournal.com** for instructions. Sorry, but we are unable to read or return submissions received by mail.

THANK YOU

We thank the following people who, by subscribing before the first issue or by donating, have financially supported *Relief*.

WE OWE EXTRAORDINARY GRATITUDE TO OUR DONORS:

HEROES:
HEATHER ACKMANN
ROBERT AND LAURA BAKER
THE MASTER'S ARTIST @ HTTP://WWW.THEMASTERSARTIST.COM

FRIEND:
CHARMAINE MORRIS

AND TO THE REST OF OUR FOUNDERS, WHO HAVE HELPED US TO MAKE THIS JOURNAL A REALITY:

VASTHI ACOSTA
ADRIENNE ANDERSON
KARI L. BECKEN
JILL BERGKAMP
STEVE BOGNER
SUSAN BOYER
SUSAN H. BRITTON
SHAWN COHEN
JONATHAN D. COON
CHAD COX
JEANNE DAMOFF
DIANNA DENNIS
BEN DOLSON
STEVE ELLIOTT
CHRISTOPHER FISHER
DEEANNE GIST
DEBORAH GYAPONG
SYLVIA HARPER
APRIL HARRISON
MATTHEW HENRY
GINA HOLMES
LEANNA JOHNSON
JILL KANDEL
MICHAEL KEHOE
BILL AND PEGGIE KRUEGER
ALLISON LEAL
DAVID LONG
JEROMY MATKIN
ANDREW MEISENHEIMER
CHRISTOPHER MIKESELL
CHARMAINE MORRIS
MARGARET M. MOSELEY
SARAH NAVARRO
NANCY NORDENSON
KAREN T. NORRELL
RANDY PERKINS
SHANNA PHILIPSON
CALEB ROBERTS
SUZAN ROBERTSON
CHRISTINA ROBERTSON
LISA SAMSON
LANDON SANDY
AOTEAROA EDITORIAL SERVICES
MICHAEL SNYDER
CATHERINE STAHL
DOROTHEE SWANSON
AMBER TILSON
SHERRI TOBIAS
PHIL WADE
DAVID WEBB
CHRISTINA WEEKS
REBEKAH WILKINS-PEPITON
MARYANNE WILIMEK
MANKATO
AND THOSE WHO PREFER TO REMAIN ANONYMOUS

If you would also like to help keep the journal going, please visit our website, www.reliefjournal.com and click on Support The Cause.

TABLE OF CONTENTS

FROM THE EDITOR'S DESK KIMBERLY CULBERTSON AND LISA OHLEN HARRIS	6
COACH'S CORNER COACH CULBERTSON	8

EDITOR'S CHOICE

HALL RAISING POETRY BY BRIAN SPEARS	10
THE LAST THING BEFORE DIRT FICTION BY MELANIE HANEY	17
THE ARK CREATIVE NONFICTION BY MIKE DURAN	23

FICTION

HIDING JUNED SUBHAN	32
THE PEGASUS LANDING ZACHARY DAVIS	56
FACES SHELLY DRANCIK	66
WHEN I WAS TWELVE STACY BARTON	73
MIDRIFT LYN HAWKS	94

CREATIVE NONFICTION

ON EARTH AMY LETTER	47
LETTERS HOME FROM SUNSHINE MOUNTAIN JILL NOEL KANDEL	82
WAITING RYAN GRAUDIN	115
MEMORIAL DAY DEANNA HERSHISER	129

POETRY

FRUIT OF THE VINE JAY RUBIN	30
TUMORS JAY RUBIN	31
CHAPLAIN NOTES DAVID BREEDEN	42
BEING SOMEWHERE DAVID BREEDEN	44
SEXT, FEBRUARY 25, 2007 DARREN J. N. MIDDLETON	45
JAPANESE PILGRIMAGE DARREN J. N. MIDDLETON	46
LOVE ANN IVERSON	52
SUNFLOWERS ANN IVERSON	53
AFTER PAINTING ANN IVERSON	54
SOLSTICE NEARING ANN IVERSON	55
WALKING BACK TO THE FERRY, BÜYÜKADA JENNIFER G. STEWART	62
ALL SAINTS' DAY, ISTANBUL JENNIFER G. STEWART	63
AMERICAN DREAM JUSTIN RYAN BOYER	64
DAFFODILS LARRY D. THOMAS	68
HE CLOTHES THEM LARRY D. THOMAS	69

IN SIN SO CRAFTILY MORTAL LARRY D. THOMAS	71
DAYLIGHT SAVINGS ED HIGGINS	72
GRACE AMANDA MCQUADE	79
STORY OF A TREE ELIZA KELLEY	80
PATER NOSTER DON THOMPSON	89
PARADIS MARTHA SERPAS	109
NOW HILL MARTHA SERPAS	110
EPITHALAMIA MARTHA SERPAS	111
THE PUZZLE OF NAMES MARC HARSHMAN	113
CANDLEMAS MARC HARSHMAN	114
A LENTEN MEDITATION GINA MARIE MAMMANO V.	119
WHISTLER SHANNA POWLUS WHEELER	120
TWO OF EVERY KIND LYNN DOMINA	121
FIRST MORNING IN HEAVEN LYNN DOMINA	122
ANTIQUE SHOP LYNN DOMINA	123
APOSTATE'S CHALLENGE LYNN DOMINA	125
MARRIAGE AFTER WAR: A FRUITFUL QUESTION NATASHA LYNN HELLER	126

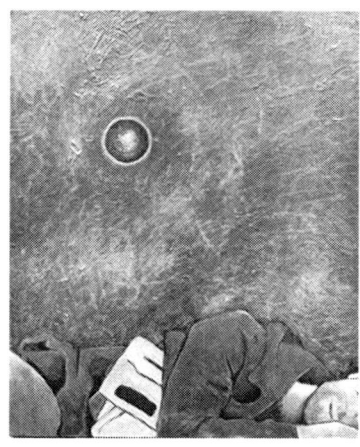

COVER ART

THIS ISSUE'S COVER ART, "JESSE AND THE MYSTICAL MAGICAL MOMENT WITH AMBROSE," IS PROVIDED BY JOSHUA BARKEY. SEE MORE OF HIS WORK AT WWW.BARKINGREED.COM. ABOUT THIS PIECE, JOSHUA SAYS, "JESSE THOUGHT THAT HIS CONSCIOUS MIND WAS BLOCKING HIS ACCESS TO AMBROSE. HE TOOK SOME PILLS, FELL ASLEEP, AND HAD A DREAM. THEN HE WOKE UP."

PLUS!

LOOK FOR A BONUS STORY, "THE DENIAL," BY MAGGIE STIEFVATER AT THE END OF THE JOURNAL. YOU'LL ENJOY THE PREVIEW OF THE SECOND EDITION OF *COACH'S MIDNIGHT DINER*, THE GENRE ANTHOLOGY COMING IN 2008 FROM CCPUBLISHING.

FROM THE EDITOR'S DESK KIMBERLY CULBERTSON
WITH LISA OHLEN HARRIS

We lost our innocence in the Fall and our return to it is through the Redemption which was brought about by Christ's death and by our slow participation in it. Sentimentality is a skipping of this process in its concrete reality and an early arrival at a mock state of innocence, which strongly suggests the opposite.
—Flannery O' Connor

I GET A LITTLE NERVOUS around people who are constantly "blessed." *How was your day today?* I ask. *Blessed*, they respond, every day and with the same faux enthusiasm. I get that every day one is allowed to breathe is a blessing and God does daily bless us in myriad ways—but no one can possibly be happy all the time; some days are bound to be harder than others. I find myself wondering whom they are trying to convince: Me? Themselves? God? It's not that I don't like happy people, or that I'm intrinsically cranky (though I'll admit I sometimes complain about the small stuff more than I should). It's that these overwhelmingly happy saints paint the Christian life to be so easy that it seems, well, fake. I crave authenticity, and I'd rather deal with devastating, raw, even angry emotion than navigate a person's forced joy.

My feelings about fiction mirror this sentiment. *Relief* attempts to meet a need for those who find stereotypical Christian literature too formulaic, too easy. They are sick of simplistic conversions and happy endings. The well-meaning have explained that Christian literature should always resolve in joy, conversion, or, in the very least, obvious consequences for the rebellious. But Flannery O'Connor calls this weakness, explaining, "It is when the individual's faith is weak, not when it is strong, that he will be afraid of an honest fictional representation of life, and when there is a tendency to compartmentalize the spiritual and make it resident in a certain type of life only, the sense of the supernatural is apt gradually to be lost."

FROM THE EDITOR'S DESK

When Christian writing insists on happy endings, we may be missing the long, slow march to the cross. It's tempting to jump to the new heavens and new earth, to ignore the long struggle of living out the salvation of a redeemed spirit through a still sinful body and into a fallen world. In fact, Satan tempted Jesus to call down angels, to head straight for the "happy ending." Instead, Jesus faced the cross and the sorrow with dignity. The Father left His Son in the tomb for days and nights while His people despaired. And though Christ's story has a joyous ending, not every chapter ends happily. Some leave off with haunting sorrow, as in Luke's account of the rich man walking sadly away.

The work in this issue contains a constant thread of death, burial, and sometimes resurrection. In some of the work, stages of death and burial are portrayed while resurrection is still but a possibility. In reality, the path to the cross and our subsequent soul work is often wrought with pain and disappointment, doubt and questions. Paul says that, "tribulation produces perseverance, and perseverance, character, and character, hope." But it is not always easy to derive hope from tribulation. It seems easier, at times, to feel hopelessness and bitterness in the face of tribulation. Ideally, trouble and pain bring people to God, but in real life, and in this issue, these troublesome seasons occasionally result in a person turning from God. There may be a spark of hope that they might someday find redemption, but it's not guaranteed—there are times when only hopelessness and loss remain. But don't give yourself over to depression; as in life, there is a great deal of redemption present in this issue as well.

As in past issues, we have chosen to showcase a piece from each genre by honoring the author with the "Editor's Choice Award." In this issue, we offer our congratulations to Brian Spears for his poem "Hall Raising," Melanie Haney for her story "The Last Thing before Dirt," and Mike Duran for his essay "The Ark." We also present the wonderful story "Letters Home from Sunshine Mountain" by Jill Noel Kandel, who graciously guest-edited our creative nonfiction for this round. Her story reflects her keen style and examines her own unnervingly cheery persona when faced with trial.

May we all recognize the long road to the cross and find hope in tribulation, but in the moments when hope is absent, may we respect rather than edit reality.

O'Connor, Flannery, "The Church and the Fiction Writer," *America* 180, no. 13 (1999): 10-14.

COACH'S CORNER COACH CULBERTSON

AN ANCIENT CHINESE CURSE STATES, "May you have an interesting life." Well, whether we believe it's a curse or a blessing (we change our minds frequently . . .), life around *Relief* is most definitely interesting. Here's what's going on in a nutshell:

I'm working on a new web store integrated into the *Relief* store, all 256-bit encrypted and nicely wrapped into the whole site. However, building a store is not the easiest thing in the world, and is taking a bit longer than I expected. Once it's done, though, we'll have a store with more features that is easier to navigate, and we'll be ready for the next thing on my list.

Ebooks are becoming a bigger and bigger deal, and we at *Relief* are quite interested in the trend. The new web store will also support downloadable ebooks for instant gratification, so you can get *Relief* as fast as your ISP's download rate will allow. *Coach's Midnight Diner: The Jesus Vs. Cthulhu Edition* will be available as an ebook as well.

Last but not least, the second edition of *Coach's Midnight Diner* is getting ready for layout. As I type this, my crack team of editors are wrapping up the edits. I can honestly say that, as proud as I am of the first *Diner*, this next edition raises the level of intensity and sets an even higher standard for Christian genre writing. Maggie Stiefvater's "The Denial" will provide you with a sneak peek of what you can expect. Look for the second volume of *Coach's Midnight Diner* in October of this year.

So that's the news for now. Check you next time!

Your friendly neighborhood tech guy,
Coach Culbertson

RELIEF | A QUARTERLY CHRISTIAN EXPRESSION
CONGRATULATES THE WINNERS OF ITS
EDITOR'S CHOICE AWARDS

<u>POETRY</u>
BRIAN SPEARS
HALL RAISING

<u>FICTION</u>
MELANIE HANEY
THE LAST THING BEFORE DIRT

<u>CREATIVE NONFICTION</u>
MIKE DURAN
THE ARK

HALL RAISING BRIAN SPEARS

I.

We drove I-10 across the lake,
    through New Orleans and beyond,
        through Kenner to Airline Highway,

past Norco's refineries,
    Hahnville High's football game,
        northwest along the river road

through twinned towns connected
    levee to levee by steel drawbridges,
        by family names and shrimp boats—

Reserve and Edgard,
Lutcher and Gramercy.

All night we drove so we could build
    a house of God for brothers and sisters
        we'd not yet met. We drove to make

a miracle happen, to raise a church
    from slab to sacrament in just two days.
        We drove to Convent.

II.

First, a prayer of blessing, a prayer
for sun and spirit to provide witness,

HALL RAISING

then clash of hammers on nails,
ninety strong, around the perimeter

of concrete slab, I on the east wall
back to the sun, ready to nail

top plate to stud every sixteen inches,
already marked, brother-strangers

either side of me ready for same.
The call to lift east wall into place

nine minutes after first strike,
pride that our wall was first up.

III.

Church, from the Greek *kyriake* by way of Germany before they were Christians, house of the Lord. Part of the pun that Jesus played on Cephas (*sefa*, Syriac for "stone" became the Latin *petrus* and thence Cephas became Peter. Puns don't work so well in translation, but that Jesus liked wordplay helps us know Him more fully.), that Jesus would build his church upon that rock of Peter's stubbornness. Words become cheated of meaning over time and disgrace and have unwelcome connotations. Churches sold the truth of Christ for lands and temporal authority, even though He'd told his apostles, "My kingdom is not of this world." Churches are corrupt, congregations* not, and we are purest of the pure. Kingdom Halls, so we don't lose sight of the most important thing and trade it for ephemera. Our eyes on future promise, on kingdom realized.

*Latin *congregare*, which Tyndale used for the Greek *ekklesia* and thus had reformer heritage. We consider Tyndale one of us, a martyr of the true congregation at the hands of apostates.

IV.

Ten-penny nails, galvanized steel,
for conjoining studs and plates,
roof trusses to raised walls.

A practiced carpenter drives them
home with three shots, one to set,
one to plunge it toward the wood,
one to sink the head below surface.
Square-headed tacks, tar-paper
into the plywood roof, to be covered
with shingles, set by chalk line
and quarter-inch roofing nails,
short, to attach, not puncture.
Sheetrock nails same, but longer,
with wide, circled heads
that broke through paper to chalk
only to be mudded over
by the crew that followed us.

V.

Rooftop, kneeling under July's humid
mid-Saturday sun, the graveled black
stuck to denim kneecaps, the heat glib
and dank. Eight feet apart, two men with chalk

strike a blue line—the leading edge of my
shingle will trace it; the left abuts
the one placed by Jeanne, Sister
Arceneaux, I mean, from Carencro.

She sets and drives her tacks with precision,
two blows for each. My first tack ricochets
under my chin, second strike just pinches
finger-skin between nailhead and flatface.

I'm sure I'll have a blister, but just now,
it would take a miracle for me to look.

HALL RAISING

VI.

Brother Bullhorn asks for hammers
to stop for just a moment; *dinner*,
he calls, and we stream out to look
at what we've wrought, and then

to eat what our new local friends
have made. Jambalaya, a hundred
gallons it seems, no skimping
on the chicken and shrimp,

a grill twenty feet long with burgers,
andouille, cob-corn sizzling. Sun
still high over our work; its descent
won't stop us, though most

will move indoors where unrocked
ceilings show insulation and conduit,
wires red, black, and green extruding
like anemones. We mount toilets,

lay formica, hang cases to hold
Bibles, songbooks, *Truth* books,
step outside for coffee, biscuit.
Moonglow blocked by a church

that wasn't there this morning.

VII.

Long lens and notebook,
      at the corner of Bishop
           and Lafourche Streets. He waves.

He's kin, I think. *We both spread
     news to those who need to hear.*
         His news, he tells me, laughing,

is the Bordelon mausoleum,
     is how Tommy Lavigne saw
         the Virgin in his cane field

and now sells tickets, the proceeds
     to put in a new wood gym floor
         at Our Lady of Divine Succor.

I tell him you see lots of things
     when you stare at the sun all day,
         but here you see God's hand

at work in the line of sisters
     passing bricks hand to hand,
         tearing down one altar

and raising another close
     to the brothers who set bricks
         in mortar, tap with trowel,

scrape excess and set the next,
     build into the wall a sign,
         a watchtower.

VIII.

She is beautiful, stretches upward
into the pre-dawn. Coffee thick
as burned roux at the corner

of the parking lot where next week

HALL RAISING

Esther and Ti-Jean and their four kids
will scurry inside to beat the rain,

Ti-Jean nervous about being the first
Watchtower reader in the new Hall.
Muffled hammer taps through the wall,

a roly-poly trundles to the concrete's edge,
tumbles, balled up into the grass-dew
where this afternoon we'll plant a hedge.

Sister Arceneaux stands, asks about
my finger, tuts over the blister. *You hear
about the next one? In September,*

*Breaux Bridge congregation. I'm sure
your finger'll be better by then.*

IX.

It's a form of service, creating this,
as much as preaching door to door.
The spirit compels us to witness

in many forms, to bring eternal bliss
to everyone. Just mopping the floor
is a form of service. Creating this

house in two days brought a witness
to those who never answer the door.
The spirit compels us to witness

even when, especially when it's senseless
to think there's time left in this wicked world
for any form of service to create this

paradise we hope our Lord Jesus
will usher in. This house we've given you, Lord.
The spirit compels us to witness

the glories you have made, your wondrous
works, the paradise you'll restore.
It's in your service we've created this.
Your spirit compels us to bear witness.

X.

That house may stand a hundred years,
may outlive me for all I know.
We built it strong enough to stand
the Devil's breath.
                                                   But now

I don't believe the Devil breathes,
don't count on paradise, don't live
for future possibility,
don't think that I will be revived

to walk with elephants and lions.
Paul said that *when I was a child,
I spake as one, and thought as one.*
Who knew that I'd consider my

disruption from the faith as my
commencement, graduation to
a fuller life. I'm proud of that
building, although I'll never go

through its doors again. At times
I catch myself whistling the psalms
we sang: *This house we built for you
Oh Lord, this house we built for you.*

THE LAST THING BEFORE DIRT MELANIE HANEY

I STOP AND THE WHOLE TABLE STOPS. Silverware hovers; forks ooze maple syrup in long amber strings. The waitress comes back around and tops off our mugs. I acknowledge her with the polite nod she deserves for coming back even though we only ordered the bare minimum, have drunk through two or three pots of free refills, and don't intend to leave her more than a dollar fifty for a tip. Yet, I'm the only one to give her the polite nod and half smile she's earned. Everyone else is still staring. At me. Their eyes like goblets, wide and rimmed with disbelief.

I put down my fork and squint over at Rusty. He's a mean looking one, lines running down between his bushy eyebrows like he's always pissed off at something. He could be holding a baby or petting a puppy, doesn't matter; the lines are always there, making people nervous. He puts his fork down too, right there on top of his half-eaten pancakes, and says to me, his mustache twitching, "So, what's this all about?"

I don't answer. The question is sort of rude, I think, considering I'm the one who invited them here for breakfast, the one who's paying for their hash browns, their pancakes, the little paper cups of whipped butter. Didn't anyone ever teach them to be thankful?

Next to him is Catherine. She has polished off at least a pot of coffee all on her own and her legs are bouncing beneath the booth—I can feel the vibrations across the floor. She hasn't said a word, just keeps staring at me with those brown saucer eyes.

I'm thinking that if anyone has the right to be asking questions, it's her.

Or really, come to think of it, it's me. I'm the one they left for dead, after all.

IT WAS THREE YEARS AGO, mid-August. We were stupid drunk and they buried me in the pitch of night. I woke with dirt in my mouth, caked-up my nostrils, cool and soft on my eyelids.

We'd fought; I remember that much. Catherine and I rolling on the sand, spitting and cursing, so close and fervent that we couldn't even see each other anymore and we might as well have been wrestling with God.

It'd been coming for a while, I knew that much. You can't be like we were—all fire all the time—without having some sort of explosion. I just wasn't counting on Rusty to come running down the beach in his saggy overalls and have me off with a shovel. The last thing I remember before dirt was his howling cry cutting into the spinning dark.

"Dammit Carl!"

Luckily for me, they were in a hurry and drunk themselves, because they did a shoddy job of burying me. When I woke up, I could see specks of daylight like stars poking through the earth. It took me less than a minute to pull myself up, blink it out of my eyes, and cough it from my lungs. But it stayed beneath the crescents of my nails for days. A thin brown line that I couldn't reach.

AT THE DINER I SMILE at Catherine. She's a little thicker than I remember, in the spread of her hips, the softness of her arms. But it looks good on her. She was all elbows and knees when we'd been together. She doesn't smile back.

"I'm here to make amends," I start to say but am interrupted.

"We went back for you," Catherine blurts, startling us all. Rusty even stops staring at me for a minute to look at her like she's crazy. Like she should just keep sipping coffee and shut up.

"In the morning, first thing," she says quickly and then shrinks back into the orange booth cushion.

Rusty shakes his head and pushes his plate to the middle of the table. "Ignore her," he says.

Impossible. I don't know much about what's going on in this town now, not since I *died* and all, but back when I was living here, Catherine was like the moon, and we all moved for her like the tide.

I eye her again, but she isn't looking at me anymore. She's nose down, lost in her mug.

WHEN YOU WAKE UP WITH DIRT UP YOUR NOSE, hung over and left for dead by the woman you thought you loved, something's got to change. You cannot just dig yourself out from the ground and go on as though life is good.

As for me, I shook the dust off my hair and hitched a ride as far away as possible.

Three towns over, I was dropped off at a truck stop and told that there would be showers, hot food, and even laundry machines. The driver thought I was homeless and put a twenty in my palm as I shook his hand outside of the cab. As I undressed in the grungy tiled bathroom, dropping all I had left in the world on the floor, I realized that he wasn't so far off.

When I came out from the showers, I headed downstairs and found myself a booth at the sparsely populated Country Buffet and told the waitress I'd have a coffee and to keep it coming.

A hulk of a man lumbered in when I was on my third or fourth mug. He sat at the counter and ordered fast, like he knew the menu. After the waitress flipped her pad shut and walked back to the kitchen, he glanced over his shoulder at me, the only other guy in the place.

He nodded and asked, "You new?"

I thought about it for a minute and then nodded. "Yup."

I supposed that I was.

"You play Scrabble?"

The question caught me off guard and I stared at him blankly until he pulled the board game from the pack on the stool beside him.

"The game." He held it up and waved it. "You play?"

His hands were massive, Frankenstein fists. The game looked like nothing more than a greeting card in his palm.

I think I laughed but shook my head. Scrabble was my grandma's game, an old people game, like bridge. Then I remembered that Catherine used to play, sometimes. She was pretty good too, played with her mother and aunts on Sunday afternoons and would then come to me and tell me that you can spell kiss with a Q and one S and it's even better than the real thing, points wise.

"But it's not even the same thing," I would tell her, and then she'd tell me to shut up and she'd slide her hand up my thigh.

"You want to learn?" The man stepped down from the vinyl stool and slid himself into the bench across from me. I didn't answer because I sort of got the feeling that he wasn't really asking as he popped the lid off with his gorilla fingers and unfolded the board between us.

"I bring it with me on the road," he said, dropping the last of the wooden tiles into the silver pouch. "Keeps my mind sharp."

He took his hat off, showing a sunburnt scalp, speckled with freckles. I leaned back in my seat, felt the vinyl of the booth pinch beneath my thighs and thought, what the hell? I have nowhere else to be.

"So what's your story?" he asked while arranging his tiles—tiles that were like the size of his nail beds. Seriously, monster hands.

"Well, I woke up dead this morning," I said. "And now here I am."

"Fair enough," he said. "You can go first."

His name was Chuck. We played four games that night. When it was over and he was getting up to leave, he asked where I was headed next.

I shrugged, hadn't thought that far ahead.

"C'mon," he said. "I know where you can get a couch. It ain't much, but it's better than here."

Chuck's sister lived just on the edge of town in a green house that looked like it was lopsided, half of it sinking into the overgrown lawn. There was a chain-link fence around it that had rusted and I couldn't figure out if it was put there to keep something in or out. Either way, it was nothing more than a rusted ornament when I got there.

CATHERINE HASN'T LOOKED AT ME since Rusty told me to ignore her. She's been picking at her cuticles.

"I play Scrabble now," I tell her. "I'm pretty good too. I mean, we go to tournaments and stuff."

She looks up at me, they both do, but like I'm crazy. Like I came back from the dead to tell them that I understand the thrill of a triple word score BINGO.

JOAN, CHUCK'S SISTER, WAS AN ER NURSE who worked overnights. Her boyfriend, Ed, didn't work. He drank some, played some cards, and spent his nights out. Sometimes he wouldn't get home until just before she did.

Joan's kids were all grown and had left, but their rooms were still set up like they might be coming back. I wasn't allowed in either of them. But she was nice enough, let me sleep on her couch and eat her food and use her bathroom.

On the third day after my burial, Joan came home from work and jostled me awake. The sun was just coming up and she smelled like Neosporin and coffee and cigarettes. She touched my shoulder and asked, "You want to make some money?"

They were hiring at her hospital and she'd put a word in for me. Transport. Just move the people from their rooms to their procedures. No degree required or anything. Of course, sometimes you had to move sick bodies, people really sick. Still, that was better than the dead ones. Either way, I had to take it. Joan got me dressed in one of her son's funeral or wedding outfits and I got the job.

So, that was my new life. Sleeping on a couch, wheeling gurneys of sick or dead people, and playing Scrabble. Joan played too. She and Chuck and I would play when he came through town, and on Thursday nights, we played in a league. We played in tournaments even, like bowling but with consonants.

The league met in the basement of a little church. And sometimes there would be pressure, you know, to come back for services on Sundays. Mostly from this guy named Bill, who BINGO'd more than anyone I'd ever met, and who swore that he had been saved from his raging alcoholism and that God had fixed the mess he'd made of his life. That God had given him a new perspective on everything.

Joan always had the excuse of work—church was past her bedtime. Chuck had the excuse of being on the road most of the time. I had nothing. So, even though I told him I already had my own perspective, I could go. *Once*.

Joan and Chuck, even Ed who'd never even met Bill, they all laughed when they heard he'd gotten to me and I was going. I hadn't been to any church since Catherine and I first started dating.

SHE HAD GROWN UP IN THE CHURCH but when we first started dating she was already falling away fast. Mostly into me. We were idiots in love, fumbling all over each other in the high school auditorium, in the AV utility room, tangled in the black coils of extension cords.

"This is male, this is female," she'd giggle, holding up the cords, showing how they connected, until I knocked them out of her hand and dragged us both to the ground.

But I didn't make her fall from grace. If it hadn't been me, it would've been some other guy. So I don't feel bad for what she and I did behind God's back. Besides, before too long she was doing Rusty behind both of our backs. He was sliding all over her on the bed of his truck, touching her just like me.

BILL'S CHURCH WAS DIFFERENT than anything I'd ever seen. For starters, there was no kneeling, no secret handshakes or crossing or repeating of words in the solemn tone of a funeral. There was even a band singing up on the stage (yes, a stage), with a guitar and drums and everything. The lead singer was wearing ragged-looking jeans and a loose green t-shirt with a faded four-leaf clover on the front and singing the same chorus over and over again, *Fire rain down*. With the smile on his face, you'd think he was singing about love.

After the service, Bill took me back to his apartment for lunch and it was amazing. Not the lunch, but the apartment. Two big bedrooms, a giant television, a clean white kitchen.

"Nice place," I told him.

"Yeah, this is where I cleaned myself up," he said and pulled a loaf of pumpernickel bread out of his fridge. "Unfortunately, my roommate just got married a couple of months ago, and I thought I could swing it, but now it's pretty tight."

I didn't blink or even breathe. All I could think was *ask me. Ask me. Ask me.*

And when he didn't, when he kept right on making sandwiches with curls of shaved ham and deli-sliced American cheese, when he kept smoothing his knife over and over and over the globs of Miracle Whip, I just blurted it out—"I could help out. I could move in."

And so I did. Joan helped me move my stuff, what little there was, and promised to come over and visit, even though Bill said she couldn't smoke in the apartment.

"You know you're going to have to go to church with him now," she told me. And she was right.

Every Sunday, *Fire rain down* and *Praise the Lord*. But I have a place to live and food to eat and friends who don't knock me unconscious and bury me alive.

THIS WHOLE MEETING UP WITH RUSTY AND CATHERINE was Bill's idea. He thought it might help me to make amends with my past, to confront it and then let it go.

"Forgiveness is powerful," he told me.

Outside the diner, I'm not so sure. They're still eyeing me like I'm about to pull a gun or call the cops, or like they're thinking they should do one or the other. Catherine puts lip gloss on for about the fourth time since she finished her last cup of coffee. She keeps sucking her bottom lip in and chewing.

"I just wanted to let you guys know that I'm in a better place," I tell them. They start to walk off. Rusty shakes his head and tells me not to call him again, ever. Catherine looks at me, but then quickly turns away and does a double step to catch up to Rusty, who's already opening the door to his side of their pickup. The engine starts and revs and I walk to my car.

"Hey Carl," Catherine calls across the parking lot. "What's the best bingo you've ever had?"

I hold my hand up over my brow, shielding my eyes from the sun so that I can see her face. She's smiling, really smiling. I tell her the best one ever, the one that I played and thought of her afterward.

"Thanks," she says. "For breakfast."

Then she ducks into the cab and the door closes. They don't pass me on their way out of the parking lot.

THE ARK MIKE DURAN

Neon lights frame a faux wooden cross. It rises behind a man who's hunched over a cigarette, working at the yellowed nub with the type of ferocity that only another addict would recognize. As he drains the final strands of tobacco, the tattoo on his neck inflates, revealing an angry Chinese dragon uncoiling from under his flannel.

A steady drizzle has left the walkway shimmering. As my wife and I negotiate a puddle and approach the illustrated man, I nod toward him.

He drops the butt and grinds it, sizzling, under his boot. "What's the word, boss?"

"The word?" I squint into the watery, gray sky. "Storm's coming, I guess."

A wry smile reveals meth-ravaged teeth. "Ever since I can remember."

I was baptized in a mountain stream in 1980. Having skinny dipped in the same pool and nestled beer cans in its icy water, it seemed only fitting that the secluded gorge be put to better use. Jesus had rescued me from an alcoholic father, a drug habit, and an existential spiral. So when my friend, another born-again ex-doper, stood across from me shivering in the glacial baptismal and asked me if I promised to follow Christ for the rest of my days, I could only answer in the affirmative. And in the name of the Father, the Son, and the Holy Spirit, the journey began.

A lot would happen in the next six years—marriage, three children, a new job. But amidst the change, God remained the constant. Back then, I got the best seat at every Bible study and wasn't afraid of breaking the ice, even if I used a sledge hammer to do so. I ordered Chick tracts by the bundle and christened the Pope as the Antichrist. The edict did not sit well with my parents, but they were on their way to hell, so what did it matter? Door-to-door evangelism became a regular weekend event and at the small church we attended, it earned me props, even if it failed to net any converts. Eventually, wisdom won out and I mellowed. Soon I was asked to join the leadership team, ordained and, before long, nominated to plant a sister church. With the rest of my high school buddies barreling toward prison, transience, or addiction, becoming a pastor was an upgrade. At the least, it was ballsy.

In July of 1986, twenty-four adults gathered at a small Baptist church for our inaugural service. The building was a testament to malaise; swollen doors teetered on creaky hinges, and cobwebs laden with insect husks draped the eaves. Velvet burgundy curtains shut out the sun like a submarine hull, giving the tiny sanctuary all the warmth of a mausoleum. As part of our lease agreement, we promised to clean the place up, hang some new doors, and revive the dead crab grass. However, demolition was the only reasonable option.

We were a ragtag bunch—David's misfit army, I always thought—an immature but zealous group, led by the chief of sinners. There were conversions, recommitments, and prophetic utterances. Times were good. The nursery was full and idealism reigned.

No wonder I didn't see the storm clouds looming.

WE LEAVE THE TOOTHLESS MAN cackling at the entrance. "Come as you are" has become a motto of mine, even if the "as you are" part includes tats, tobacco, ear awls, and assorted addictions. Dragging chords of nicotine into a warm foyer, we pass unusually helpful, bulletin-wielding volunteers into the sanctuary. We sit about halfway back, close enough to appear interested but far enough away to avoid looking like groupies. Of course, I must have the aisle seat. Whether it's because I'm claustrophobic or antisocial, I still can't bring myself to be surrounded by God's people. Perhaps it's a hangover from eleven years in the ministry.

Islands of congregants punctuate oceans of empty pews, so there are plenty of aisle seats still to choose from. The weather is keeping folks away. When one's livelihood depends on putting butts in the seats, this internal stat counter can become a tyrant. Nowadays, however, I am nothing more than a butt in the seat, so the stat counter and the sparse crowd are not nearly as onerous as they used to be.

We find a spot near an adulterer. This is not a moment of clairvoyance on my part or an ad-hoc judgment, for I know the man. Once a paragon of conjugal know-how, he is recently divorced and, for reasons known only to his ex, believes that oral sex is, technically, not sex. Despite the dissolution of a twenty-one-year marriage, he's assured us of God's mercy and the future's glow, neither of which I can deny.

I struggle through worship, not because of the adulterer's proximity or the woman behind me who cannot hold a note, but because, despite the peppy chorus, Jesus is not my "all in all" and singing so only enflames my culpability. So at the risk of appearing aloof, I opt to sit this one out.

Meanwhile, the sprinkle outside has become a shower, and inside the stink is growing.

* * *

DO NOT ENTER THE MINISTRY *if you can help it.* That was Charles Spurgeon's advice to his pupils. He wrote, "If any student in this room could be content to be a newspaper editor, or a grocer, or a farmer, or a doctor, or a lawyer, or a senator, or a king, in the name of heaven and earth let him go his way." Despite my options—or lack thereof—I had barreled recklessly into the ministry. But after a few years, I began wishing I'd heard Spurgeon's admonition sooner.

Within a year of starting the church, we added another child to our family and the congregation doubled in size. It was more a testament to God's grace than anything. I hadn't attended seminary or studied the "church growth" experts enough to know what I was doing wrong. And when I did err, the faithful were more than willing to wink at my youth. Yet the facility's leaky faucets and crumbling asphalt quickly got old. Eventually, the church relocated to an elementary school. The bright, boomy confines of the cafeteria were a stark contrast to the crypt we'd been hunkered in. It gave us some legroom and a notion of progress. Before long we had cracked the hundred-member mark. and a sense of possibility, however illusory, tainted our collective psyche.

I hit my stride as a preacher and poured myself into sermon crafting. Gone were the days of high school delinquency and life without purpose; the gifts that had lain dormant under generations of spiritual sediment sprang to life. God had called me to speak! But like Moses, I had to descend the mountain to do so. And whatever glow I'd acquired from communing with God faded quickly in the service of his people.

Author Frederick Buechner wrote that God chooses "for His holy work in the world . . . lamebrains and misfits and nitpickers and holier-than-thous and stuffed shirts and odd ducks and egomaniacs and milquetoasts and closet sensualists." I had never mistaken God's family for the Cleaver clan, but becoming the default arbiter between the Beave and Wally got to be taxing. Apparently, it wasn't enough that I could recite Calvin's TULIP from memory, articulate eschatological timelines, and construct a killer three-point sermon. I also had to indulge a dysfunctional flock.

But is any flock not?

Perhaps a more seasoned minister would have been unfazed by the tedium. But the nagging drip of discontent and indifference, petty squabbles and cultural quirks, became like water torture, with each successive droplet eroding my inspiration. Like the crew on Noah's ark, I spent a lot of time shoveling shit.

Meanwhile, my beautiful bride and our four ducklings were looking for shelter because Daddy was increasingly AWOL and it was starting to rain.

AFTER WORSHIP, AN ENTHUSIASTIC ELDER REMINDS US that this is the day the Lord has made and asks us to greet the people nearby. I turn and discover that the tonality-challenged lady is also fashionably unkempt. Nevertheless, we shake hands and I commend her for her musical abandon. Thankfully, Jesus is not a respecter of musical talent or panache.

Several rows back is a friend whose wife recently died of cancer. I am privileged to have seen them both come to Christ and, one smoggy SoCal summer, baptized her in a Doughboy swimming pool. Per her request, we kept the witnesses to a minimum. Having raised three daughters on her own, she possessed a quiet, almost elegiac, resolve. It's no wonder that she declined the second round of chemo, opting instead to gut it out.

Once, near the end, I took my acoustic guitar over to their house and we sat together and sang praise songs. Then I held her and cried harder than I've ever cried in public—huge, snotty sobs, followed by a word from the Lord. She seemed embarrassed by my lack of composure. Several weeks later, I officiated her funeral. I managed to harness my emotions, but was unable—as I am now—to articulate just how much she means to me.

Her husband also prefers aisle seats and, this time, two of the girls are with him. They have struggled since their mother's passing with the youngest squandering a scholarship and the eldest getting a boob job. I cross the aisle and greet them. The man prefers handshakes to hugs; nevertheless he yields stiffly to my embrace. He quickly prods me about USC and I counter by dissing Notre Dame. Yet behind the banter, there is sadness, an ache without end. As I return to my seat and prepare for the pastor's sermon, I can't help but wonder how many other wounded hearts fill this sanctuary.

IN RETROSPECT, IT WAS A TURNING POINT, a nasty uppercut after a series of jabs.

New Year's morning 1991, as we gathered for breakfast with some friends, I received a frantic call informing me that a member of the church had just committed suicide.

Later on, I would discover that there are stages to dealing with this type of thing. Disbelief, guilt, regret, and anger are typical after someone you know takes their own life. But as I raced to the house, all of those emotions assailed me without prejudice or regard to classification.

I knew him well. We had graduated together, played basketball on weekends, met for counseling, and often discussed his battle with depression. He was seeing a therapist and had once come dangerously close to being institutionalized. A fragile, gentle soul, he was loved by many. Yet this was not enough to keep him from pulling the trigger.

It was a double-barrel shotgun, to be exact, which he fired into his left temple. On his nightstand were the pills he'd stopped taking and a book on Christians and demon possession. We had to restrain his father as the coroner took the body away, and the police confiscated the remaining guns from the premises for precaution. Three men from the church and I volunteered to clean the room. We spent the day picking particles of scalp from the acoustic texture, weeping, and wondering what had gone wrong. By evening, the room was in order, and the four of us stood around his bed, joined hands, and prayed.

Several hundred came to pay their last respects. It was standing room only. I officiated the funeral and was expected to say something timely, something to absolve us of guilt and illuminate the theological murk. Instead, I said he was a jerk and promised I'd tell him that to his face one day.

The event traumatized our church. A few members also confessed thoughts of suicide, something I learned was common to those left behind. People in the core became closer and those on the fringe drifted. Some abandoned their faith. We looked to God for wisdom, to each other for warmth. They all looked to me for strength. Little did they know, I was looking for a life preserver.

THE PASTOR TAKES THE PULPIT and I quickly give him a once-over. It's a bad habit of mine, I know. One morning, in the middle of my sermon, my wife slipped me a note that read: "Your zipper is down!" Being transparent before the congregation is hard enough without also exposing yourself. So I instinctively scan the minister to ensure his decency.

Having delivered sermons for more than a decade, listening to them is now a trying affair. Audience inattention is deplorable, as are weak intros, and I'm deft at detecting both. It's the scar from devotion to the craft, an inbred nitpickiness that prevents me from enjoying the experience. Nevertheless, I hold to the belief that sermons are like meals: meant for sustenance rather than enjoyment. I can only hope that someone, somewhere, is healthier because of a meal I made.

D. Martyn Lloyd-Jones, the great Welsh preacher, said there is no exhilaration like taking the pulpit knowing you have a word from God. Conversely, there is no feeling like standing before the congregation without one. The vacant stares, the disconnect, the unfurling panic that discombobulates and flushes you with sweat. It's like discovering your zipper is down before a crowd of snickering onlookers. I have known both these feelings.

Today's message is about a Rich Fool, which immediately lets me off the hook. Despite the listless delivery and the congregation's apparent indifference, the sermon goes well enough. During the ensuing altar call someone's cell phone shatters the sacred moment, which could explain why no one goes forward.

During my tenure, I extended my share of altar calls. Being on the other end is awkward. Perhaps it's the conviction that I could go forward every week and still not be free of this infernal stench. Like every other Sunday, I remain seated.

* * *

Somehow, like the Jews of old, what should have been a journey toward promise became a wandering in the wilderness, an incremental dying. Whether it was financial issues or facility demands, or my own spiritual density, our congregation stayed on the move. We would relocate three more times in the next five years: to a Lutheran church—night services, no less—another elementary school, and finally a community center. Rolling stones may gather no moss, but they also lose mass as they tumble. Likewise, each successive move whittled away the faithful.

The statistics are staggering. The average pastor lasts only five years at a church, and whether it's due to moral failure, spiritual burnout, or infighting among members, they leave the ministry at a rate of fifteen hundred each month. Fifty percent of pastors' marriages will end in divorce, many of them due to marital infidelity or just plain neglect. Later on, the stats would console me: I wasn't alone in this slog. However, by then, we had merged with a sister church and I was gearing up for another round.

In the back of my mind, it was a concession to failure. The idea of merging two unhealthy churches into one healthy one is akin to believing marriage will heal two screwed-up people. So while I looked forward to sharing the load with another pastor, both of us brought baggage. And the unpacking left us even more disillusioned.

I went from *senior* to *associate* pastor, but we shared the preaching load. To ease the new church's financial burdens, I went part-time and juggled various staff roles. Between throwing newspapers and coaching my kids' soccer teams, I taught Bible studies, entertained youth groups, endured staff meetings, and endless psychological autopsies.

Like blended families, merged churches bear a built-in volatility. As with gene-splicing, fusing households with different histories, visions, and values involves a high degree of difficulty. Mutations are inevitable. After several years of role-wrestling, grinding relationships, and uneven idling, it was apparent the experiment had failed. The healing I needed required more than just a new job description.

In the end, we agreed to disband the church.

The senior pastor and I tried to transition everyone the best we could, but the dismay was inevitable. Couldn't we work it out, and if not, where should they all go? Some members applauded our humility; others gave us the middle finger. Grand soliloquies gave way to over-spiritualized analyses. Some said I'd lost my saltiness, left my first love. I conceded as much. Yet the light at the end of the tunnel was way too inviting.

Eventually their hurt yielded to grace. We had come a long way from the rickety Baptist church, and shared moments of genuine joy along the way. I'd grown to love them, the lame-brains, misfits, and nitpickers. Their quirks mirrored mine. But like a bad-ass rock concert, it ended. We walked away from the trash and overflowing outhouses with a recollection of transcendence. We had partaken of something great. But in the end it came down to needs—I needed a rest and they needed more than I could give.

So we scattered—the intercessors, ushers, prophets, and parking lot attendants. All those years of faithful service, scattered like corn seed in a cow pasture. Some members transitioned seamlessly into other churches, more the wiser. Others went away carping, and still others apostatized.

Me? I began another faith journey.

WE ARE DISMISSED AND I NOTICE IT'S POURING OUTSIDE. After some pleasantries, my wife and I prepare to plunge into the deluge. As we approach the exit doors, we cross paths with a woman whose adult son has recently renounced Christianity and become an overlord in a virtual world of wizards, griffins, and talking conifers. I cannot pronounce his new name.

The woman's husband is on staff and she informs us that the church is scrambling to hire more employees. Between a messy termination, a leave of absence, a shortage of children's ministry workers, an influx of addicts, and an upcoming seminar on Spirit-filled living, the workload is becoming unmanageable.

I decline the offer for employment. Again.

We remind each other about God's faithfulness, embrace, and leave for a family luncheon that will be, most likely, far less colorful and dramatic.

"The church is like Noah's ark," said Reinhold Niebuhr. "If it weren't for the storm outside, we couldn't stand the stink inside."

It's taken me a long time to say it, but here goes: *I love the Church*—the bad, broken, two-faced, moronic, insecure children that the Father has sought out and saved. Like me. With all its flaws and faux pas, despite the bitching and back-stabbing, the Church is God's vessel, an ark in a drowning world.

And inside is the most beautiful stink.

There's a storm outside; the clouds of judgment are gathering. But God's made a way of escape. See that ark? Okay. Now hold your nose and get in.

---

p. 25: Spurgeon, Charles. *Lectures to My Students*. Grand Rapids, MI: Zondervan, 1979.
    Buechner, Frederick. Cited in Yancey, Philip. *Disappointment with God*. Grand Rapids, MI: Zondervan, 1988.
p. 27: Lloyd-Jones, D. Martyn. *Preachers and Preaching*. Grand Rapids, MI: Zondervan, 1972.
p. 29: Niebuhr, Reinhold. Cited in MacArthur, John. "The Qualities of True Love," Pt. 4. Online Study Guide: http://www.biblebb.com/files/MAC/sg1867.htm

FRUIT OF THE VINE JAY RUBIN

Cursed be Canaan!
　—Genesis 9:25

Several seasons after the flood
Noah farms a vineyard
Reaps his harvest, drinks his reward
Once drunk, passed out, alone
In his tent—his snores call out
Summon his sons: One finds nudity
Two step backward, a blanket
Tiptoed between them, a drape
To cover their father's shriveled sex

One night, millennia later: A crash
A crunch of bent metal
A sharp crack of shattered glass
The dazed driver staggers toward me
Kneels on the sidewalk, hands clasped
Help me, he prays. *Help him*, he points
A shadow beneath the headlight beams
Now, I kneel—an unconscious fool
Smelling of wine on the pavement
Beard unkempt, jeans unzipped
My jacket drapes his swollen sex

When Noah awoke to discover
The sin of his son, he cursed him
Forever a slave to his brothers
The car-struck drunk never awoke
For weeks, only his sandal remained
A fossil, a stain of shame on our street

TUMORS JAY RUBIN

But the hand of the Lord was heavy
. . . and smote them with emerods.
    —I Samuel 5:6

When Philistines stole the Hebrews' ark
Abducting their tablets, dragging them off
Hostages held in heathen hands, their scoffs
Howled louder than a pack of jackal barks
Soon, though, their fingers spread the marks
Of thievery: On their faces, splotches
Pustules, gleet; even in their crotches
Crabs and lice like rats and mice, each bite a spark
Of fire.   And what of *my* past larcenies?
A chocolate bar, a marijuana plant
A kiss, a joke my father told, a called catch
In center field. What's my curse for these?
What's my penalty? This itching, constant
Itching—and so I scratch and scratch and scratch.

HIDING JUNED SUBHAN

For Dr. John Coyle

IT WAS WIDELY RUMOURED IN THE NEIGHBOURHOOD where rumours spread from one house to the next like blood-sucking flies that his father was mad, mentally infirm, mentally deficient, a nuisance to the general public, even dangerous. That after suffering a stroke—his father had never smoked in his life—he wasn't quite the same. Luke had found him curled up in a ball on the polished kitchen floor, twitching, with soapy hands—he'd obviously been washing the dishes. There was a minor hemorrhage, a clot in the brain that healed by itself, and he did recuperate from a temporary speech impairment and paralysis. He nevertheless had a limp in his walk and was accused of speaking rudely to pedestrians, shopkeepers, traffic wardens. Children teased him and were scared of him because he had a walking stick, which he'd wave around threateningly like a crazy weapon. People thought he might be a drunkard; there were many of those around.

So when he rang Luke and was blabbering down the phone almost deliriously, ranting in broken sentences, in a concerned, gravelly voice, he understood why his father was considered insane. "Dad, what's the problem?" he asked. "You need to speak slower. I can't understand a word you're saying."

"It's gone! The damn . . . the damn thing . . . has gone . . . Luke, you have to come! Now! I can't find her!"

"Dad, who has gone?"

"The cat."

"Cat?"

"Yes, the cat! You must hurry now."

Luke sighed. "I'll be on my way."

He had to admit, he couldn't avoid it, notably when he spoke to his father who was in his seventies, that he did feel guilty about leaving him on his own. He was the one and only child in the family. He did have a spare room in his flat where his father could stay, but Luke wasn't in the flat often except to go to sleep. He wouldn't be able to care for him properly. Plus, his father was vociferous on how he felt and vehemently declared that he preferred to be in his own house—he was not prepared to move anywhere else. "This house is in my blood," he'd said. "The house goes when I go." Luke hadn't thought about that, or had he?

"Come now!" his father said.

"Alright, Dad, alright."

His father lived a little over an hour's drive away. It would be dark by the time he got there, but not very late. Luke shook his arms. He was tense. He was hoping his father hadn't caused a scene, or he'd have to go apologising to the neighbours on his behalf, which would be embarrassing.

It was 6:15 p.m. He hadn't eaten anything since midday. He could eat something when he got back.

LUKE ARRIVED OVER AN HOUR LATER, longer than he'd hoped, though he was speeding, nearly hitting 80 mph on the road. He was aware that he could have been pulled over by the police, that he could have caused a serious accident, fatally injuring himself or another driver. The ride had been a rough one.

The downstairs lights were on in the house, which was called *Silver Maple*—a name whose origin he was uncertain of. He staggered up the driveway, up to the front porch. He tapped the door and waited, quivering, then tapped again, harder, and his father eventually opened, saying, "For God's sake, can't a man have a pee in peace in his own house!"

"Hi Dad," he said, hugging him. His father's body was rigid, and Luke had to hold his breath because he smelled of antiseptic.

"Come in. I've been going mad searching for her! She's done this to me before, but she always came back. I bet she's hiding somewhere."

His father's speech was slurred, as if his tongue had been stretched. Although Luke was taller in height, his father was supposed to have resembled him in his youth. His father was once stockily built, but now, he was clenching a walking stick and his hands were square, puckered. His hair was the colour of cigarette ash, coarse-looking, and was combed to the side. His lips were thin and his brows weren't visible. He did have a limp, as though one leg were shorter than the other. Astonishingly, he managed to move with a certain amount of deftness.

"When was the last time you saw her, Dad?" he said, raising his voice. His father had disappeared into the kitchen, end of the hallway, on the right. He heard him banging his walking stick on the floor. He repeated, "Dad, when did you see her last?"

"Her name's Emerald," his father said, correcting him. "I haven't seen her since yesterday evening. She's a black cat."

His father seemed stiff, angry.

The floorboards made a squeaky sound as he moved slowly along the hallway. The smell in the house was strong, familiar. There were paintings, charcoal sketches, and pencil sketches of ships at sea on the walls. Luke remembered looking at them in a daze when he was younger. He was disappointed and there were frequent nightmares after his mother told him his father worked in a slaughterhouse where cows were suspended on tarnished hooks, and was not a fisherman as he'd imagined.

He'd never seen his father return home saturated in blood.

He tried not to breathe in too deeply. The dank house was big, with two upper floors and four large bedrooms, and he remembered stumbling down the spiral staircase when he was eight—he had wet, slippery feet, having been out of the bath (his mother had bathed him hadn't she, scrubbing him with a loofah?)—and he was naked, cold, only wrapped in a towel that had slipped off, exposing his tiny, pink genitals. He'd bruised the side of his head, and it was his father who'd picked him up like a heap of grubby laundry, as he squealed.

HE VEERED INTO THE KITCHEN. His father was clearing the table, scrunching together scraps of newspaper and disposing of them in the bin. Luke was amazed by the quickness at which his father performed the task. One of the light bulbs on the ceiling flickered. He felt dizzy. The lights were glaringly bright, and he heard a buzzing sound.

"I bet the bitch is hiding here somewhere!" his father said, swinging his walking stick. "I haven't bothered reporting this to the police. They're useless anyway . . . Do you hear that mewling? Do you?"

Luke shook his head.

"Well, I do."

He was surprised with the way his father spoke. It wasn't often that he heard him cursing; even as a child he didn't think he did. His father's skin looked bleached, the fingernails curiously long, yellow, caked with dirt, as though he'd been digging earth with his bare hands.

Luke was thinking if he'd previously seen the cat. He must have seen it. Yet, he knew he couldn't picture her properly. He believed she was black, as his father had said. But why couldn't he see her? Was she a cat with a collar-belt? Was she fat? Skinny? Did she have distinguishable footprints? There were tins of cat food on the shelves—chicken with jelly, duck breast, salmon, and tuna—along with out-of-date tins of baked beans, ham, and mackerel in brine. There was an empty tray under the sink for the cat litter. Balls of black fur were strewn on the floor.

"Why you roaming around my shelves?" his father asked reproachfully. "That's not why I called you over."

His father stared at him, puzzled, almost longingly.

"Sorry," he said, putting back on the shelf a jar of cloudy, urine-coloured pickled onions. "When did you buy her?"

His father regarded him in silence. His brows were arched, and his eyes probing, accusatory.

"I didn't *buy* her. She's a stray. You've seen her here before, remember?"

"No, I can't."

"You're acting as if you've had a stroke, not me!" his father said, snickering a little.

His father went on to say that he hadn't fed her in a couple of days, and Luke stared at the tins of cat food on the shelves.

"I hope she hasn't starved to death," he said. "She's always here with me, purring, circling round my feet, begging me to feed her. I have been good to her, Luke, and see what she does, the ungrateful bitch! I've roamed everywhere, but I'm telling you this is one of her clever jokes! I know she's lurking in a corner in the house, making that scratching sound."

Luke massaged his itchy eyes, and suddenly his father was standing in front of him—he didn't know how, he hadn't seen him move forward—seizing his arms, his face veiny and lips coated with saliva.

"You have to look for her, Luke," he said, talking rapidly, squeezing his arms. He was wearing a V-neck jumper and ragged trousers. "I'm sure she's in the house, she can't be anywhere else! I can hear her. This is one of her filthy games!"

"There's no need to get stressed, Dad," he said, taking his father's hands off his arms. "I'll go look for her." Luke told himself, *it'll be over soon . . . it will be over.*

HE SURVEYED THE LIVING ROOM, where the lights were dimmer than in the kitchen.

Luke felt hazy; his nose itched and his throat tickled. His eyes were damp and they stung a little.

The television was gone.

Two of the drawers in the glass cabinet were hanging open.

Luke said, "You say she's been missing since yesterday. It hasn't been that long, Dad. She could be back soon."

"But this isn't like her," his father replied. He stood close to him. Luke felt his breath curl up his neck. "She was prowling in the house yesterday. She was moving around the chairs, under the kitchen table, and I kept on telling her that I'd feed her if she gave me a minute, and I know I hadn't fed her in a while, but that's no reason to be mad at someone, is it? Then she was gone. But I know I heard her, she's definitely in the house. Listen . . . listen, Luke, can't you hear that scratching? That's *her*."

Luke checked behind the sofas. He saw no sign of her. He sneezed, coughed. A strange, pimply redness had formed on his wrists. Was he allergic to the cat? Twines of black fur were matted on the sofa where she'd slept. He picked up a few strands. They were thick and oddly familiar to him. He paused, then said, "She's not in here."

Luke turned around. His father's eyes were like chiselled stones, hard, glistening.

"She's done this before. Once I found her in the basement. How the hell she got in there, I don't know, but she did. She's a clever witch! She's doing this on purpose!"

There was a loud knocking on the door, and Luke nearly spluttered. He rushed to open it. It was an elderly woman on the doorstep, a woman of similar age to his father he thought. She was slim, dressed in a cardigan—beautiful in a fading, powdery way.

"Oh, I am sorry to bother you. I live next door. I heard shouting and wondered if everything was okay?"

Luke's face was flustered. "Everything is fine, Mrs. . . . ?"

"It's Jacqueline Blake." She was trying to peer over his shoulder.

He shifted to the side of the door.

"Who is it?" his father shouted. "Tell them to go away, they have no business here!" and quickly Luke said, "We're fine, Mrs. Blake. Thank you for dropping by," and before she could reply, he shut the door.

"Who was that?"

"No one, Dad."

"Why can't they leave me alone? Isn't a man allowed his own privacy? Isn't there anywhere I can go without being harassed? The bastards won't leave me alone, knocking on my door to see what I'm up to!"

"Dad," he said, like he was protesting, "you have to lower your voice. People can hear you. I'll help you look for Emerald, but you have to be quiet."

Limping away, his father said sardonically, "I'll speak however I please. They can't do anything, and neither can you."

SYSTEMATICALLY, LUKE INSPECTED THE HOUSE. After searching one area, he'd realise he'd been searching it for too long, and the absolute ridiculousness of it, of not finding her, and he'd have to start somewhere else. He'd spent nineteen of his twenty-nine years in the house, and at certain points he believed he'd never get out, that somehow he was bound to it, even ensnared by it, like a foul cage. He did believe that an indescribable force could inflict severe pain on him if he continued to stay.

He was daunted by the size of the house. Luke never knew precisely why his parents chose to purchase a huge building. There were rumours being whispered, like children's voices, in the neighbourhood about his family, rumours that his parents did not confront, rumours about miscarriages, three miscarriages, in fact, or more.

The study-room was stuffy. There was a bookshelf, a chair, a desk, a fan. He particularly noticed a photograph of his mother on the pine bookshelf. He didn't know when it was taken. She looked old, with a soft-crinkled face and baggy eyes. He couldn't see if she had shoes on beneath her plain, sleeveless dress, because a thicket of tall grass concealed her legs. There was a tiny gap in her mouth, as if she was about to utter something. Luke's mind felt muddled.

He then paced into the dining room. He circled it clockwise. The cat wasn't in there either. He didn't understand why there was a dining room, since he recalled no one ever eating in there. He had seen his mother scrupulously polishing the crystal glasses and candle holders, humming to herself while she did, but a meal was never served on the table.

Luke didn't search the bathroom, thinking that the cat would not be in there, and then again it could be. He briefly glanced around it. There was a strong chemical smell like bromine. The shower curtain was mouldy.

Switching the bathroom light off, he said, "Dad, where are you?"

"In the kitchen!"

"She's not down here."

"Have you checked upstairs?"

"I'm about to."

There was a clank. He's dropped a plate, or a cup, Luke thought, peering up the staircase. His neck and shoulders ached.

HE WENT UP THE STAIRS COURAGEOUSLY. The air struck him as chilly. He hadn't switched the light on. He had to squint in the dark. He could see fairly well where he was going. Holding the banister like a tentative child, he had his eyes on the ceiling, which seemed to increase in height and become more pointed as he walked further up.

His breathing had slowed. His chest throbbed. A streak of perspiration filtered down his neck and he scowled.

Avoiding the bathroom on the first floor, Luke opened the door to one of the two bedrooms of the four, which remained unoccupied—they were not used by his parents or anyone else. His palms were sweaty. His grip wasn't strong when he held the door handle, not as strong as it should be. It was spacious and had a mouldy odor. His father once bought bunk beds for both of them, but they were later discarded, and no reason was provided as to why he'd bought them initially.

He peered into the second bedroom. It was the dustier of the two, and draughty. The blinds were hanging askew and the windows were greasy. The moonlight oozed in cold, snaky. Luke wondered if there was a shadow hanging above him, somewhere.

His bedroom was on the second floor. It smelled acrid, like ammonia. Luke inhaled, exhaled, and inhaled again. There were blinds in the windows. The bed had only a mattress that was frayed along the sides. There was no duvet or pillows. He saw himself as a young boy of seven sitting on that bed, waiting for those breezy, creaking sounds he was convinced he'd heard to fade away. He mentioned it to his mother. "What do you hear?" his mother asked him. "Someone blubbering in the wind," he replied, and his mother told him he was being silly, why would someone be blubbering? She said he had an active imagination; it wasn't uncommon for boys of his age.

He only remembered fragmented parts of his boyhood, as if other areas had been erased. He saw the freckly boy he once was, who was now running away from him with a morose look on his face.

He touched the wallpaper. His mother must have chosen it. It was dotted with flowers. It was not the type of pattern Luke was fond of.

Luke let a few minutes pass by, switching the light off, he thought he heard something—a faint, plaintive mew—but the cat was not in his bedroom. There was no sign of the cat. He had to remind himself that it was the cat he was examining the house for.

"Emerald, are you here?" he said. "Are you in the house?"

Speedily, he shut the door. *I didn't hear anything*, he said to himself. *This is stupid. The cat cannot be here.* He was in no doubt that she had gone astray.

FINALLY, HE REACHED HIS PARENTS' BEDROOM, now only his father's. It was dank and the ground felt skewed at a crooked angle. As a child, he rarely entered his parents' bedroom but his mother didn't object if he did. Once, he saw her sitting at her dressing table, dressed in a nightgown. Her hair was loose. She was taking her clip earrings off, gazing distractedly into the mirror. The lamp was on, and her face looked glazed, delicate, like glossy paper.

The bedroom had an unpleasant odour like urine—he wondered if the cat had ventured in here. Could it have travelled up two flights of stairs? If it did, what would it be doing here?

The bed was unmade, the sheets dingy and furrowed.

The empty dressing table chair was chipped and turned sideways.

There weren't any photographs on the walls, like there used to be. His father had sealed them away, or thrown them out. There was a teakwood wardrobe in the far left corner, where his mother used to keep her clothes and shoes, and his father's ironed shirts and trousers. He was feeling discomforted. He didn't think he should be glancing around his parents' bedroom.

He didn't inspect the wardrobe, afraid of what he might not find.

"Have you found her?"

His chest heaved. His legs stiffened. Luke said, "Dad, you could have warned me. Do you always creep up on people like that?" He hadn't heard his footsteps, nor the tapping of his walking stick.

His father walked in a few steps and stopped, not too far from the doorway. He seemed vague. "She's definitely hiding. I can feel her presence."

Luke noticed his father's growing impatience.

"Dad, you could be imagining it. I've searched—"

"I don't imagine things, Luke," he said, hurt. "I know she's around. But you think I'm senile like the rest of them, don't you?"

"Dad, I don't think you're senile," he said, advancing towards him.

"Don't you?" His lips were cracked.

"No, I don't."

His father's hands were still grimy, crusted with earth.

"You have no idea, she's a deceptive little thing, always full of tricks. This is another one of her games, Luke." His eyes dilated, the pupils glinting. "She's doing this to torment me! But I know if I found her, I'd take proper care of her, and she'd never hide again."

"We'll find her, Dad," he said. He did his best to calm his father down.

"I've made some tea for us both," his father said. "Come down into the kitchen."

Turning the light off, Luke hastily scanned the room. Nothing. The moonlight slashed in through the windows, wavering.

THE TEA WAS WEAK AND SUGARY. Luke had a distaste for things that were excessively sweet. He was tentative when he'd taken the cup of tea his father had boiled for him. His father was shaking his walking stick, exuding a tinge of anger. He explained to his father, making it as clear as possible, that he doubted the cat was in the house. For a moment, Luke shut his eyes and rubbed his forehead. His earlier hunger had subsided.

"Sh-h-h-h, I heard a noise," his father said. "There's scratching, she's clawing at something, she's stuck—"

"Dad, there's no noise," he said. "You're hearing things."

"I'm not!" he said, glaring at him with a sneering curiosity. He turned towards Luke, suddenly conspiratorial.

Luke stroked his trouser belt, then rolled back the sleeves of his shirt.

"You said you didn't feed her. Where did you see her after that?"

"How the hell should I know? I don't keep a second-by-second record of things."

"But you keep saying she's here."

"She is here."

"So when did you see her last exactly?"

"I don't know!" he said. He paused, frowning. "I told you . . . it was . . . it was yesterday . . . it was yesterday evening."

For five minutes they both said nothing. His father slurped his tea and started mumbling. Luke looked at his watch. It was approaching 9:30 p.m. His father started talking about how much he disliked going shopping. Luke sat still, listening. He was perspiring. His stomach cringed. A pounding sensation ruptured through his head. As he watched his father drink, Luke remembered when his mother spilt hot, steaming cocoa over her dress. It soaked through, scalding her skin. She shrieked and her face glowed heatedly in pain, but he couldn't recollect what happened after that. He wiped his eyes.

"Dad, maybe she's been stolen," he said.

"Don't say that! D—on't say th—at."

"But it does happen."

"No it doesn't!"

The cup dropped from his father's hand. A stream of dark liquid snaked across the floor.

"What's got into you, Luke?" he said, scooping the cup up. He swabbed the tea with a sponge, then left to go to the bathroom. Luke got up from the chair to wash his hands. His fingers darkened in the water. The pimply redness had faded from his wrists. He dried his hands with a kitchen towel he tore off from a thick bundle. He was thinking that he'd aggravated his father unintentionally. He said, "Dad, do you need me for anything else whilst I'm here? I have to go soon." There was silence. "Dad?"

There was rattling in the kitchen. He was sure there was.

Luke stood stiff and colour drained out of his face. He heard the rattling again. It wasn't loud.

"Dad?" he said, "Dad, is that you?"

There was no reply. "For God's sake," he muttered, gritting his teeth.

The noise came from somewhere in the kitchen. Luke walked past the refrigerator and through to a short, narrow corridor, which led to the back garden. It was the door. It had been left open. Hadn't his father locked the door? Did he have a habit of leaving doors unlocked? After all, it wasn't safe; anyone could barge in.

He was sweating again. He was feeling muzzy.

The security lights in the garden were on full beam. He didn't require a torch, and even if he did, he'd have no clue where to find one in the house. The garden was bordered with an evergreen hedge. There was a washing line where his mother would pin up the laundry using plastic pegs, and an apple tree, a cherry tree, and weeds where flowers had blossomed. The leaves shimmered. The grass hadn't been trimmed, and it was dewy. It was a fairly extensive garden. There had been a pond once, but his father had it filled with cement and paved over it. As a child, didn't he feed the fish with flaky food?

The moon was a disc of silver. There was no breeze. His face bristled.

"Emerald," Luke said. "Where are you?"

The darkness pulsed like a blue vein.

He walked with a deliberate pace and felt a few spots of rain pepper the top of his head.

The branches poking out of the hedge looked spindly. The apple and cherry trees carried no fruit.

And there, amongst the gnarled, knobbly weeds and loose rocks, he was convinced he saw something glistening and coiled like a tail. His breath shortened and his palms were damp. A bitter taste had formed on the roof of his mouth. His tongue went dry and his toes curled in his shoes. His heartbeat thinned, declining. Luke was suddenly cold and his skin pulled in tight around his chest, close to his ribs. His vision receded, shrunk.

Behind him he heard, "What are you doing over there Luke? I told you to check inside the house. Who told you to go out?"

He bent forward, sinking into the thicket of weeds. They scoured him, thorns jabbing his skin. There was a rancid smell, like old butter. "Oh, you poor thing," he said, "you poor thing, who would dare do this to you?"

His father's thudding footsteps inched nearer towards him.

CHAPLAIN NOTES DAVID BREEDEN

1.

Patient moved to
Palliative care
Actively dying
Wife exhausted
Family has gone

2.

Pray for me, chaplain
Pray for a job on first shift
Instead of second
Pray for my child's health
Pray for a college acceptance
Pray we make it

3.

The evening and my shoes squeak
The bonhomie of the day
Snuffed into family
Wrestling with pillows
Doctors a bit louder—
"His veins all suck"
"There's a hundred procedures for that"
Cops escorting a gurney
A man with bullet holes
The day's pretense
To cover a corpse gone

4.

Paged to bless mom
Bless her in her coma
"I'm Methodist" says
The daughter, "but Momma
She's still Catholic."

5.

"My husband and I
We built that church—
Our names are on
The cornerstone there—
My husband, he was the
First funeral there."

6.

Woman with a tracheotomy
Scribbles across a notepad

I want to die
Why don't I die?
Why don't I die?
I want to die

7.

I do the Rite of the Dead
Woman praying with me
Alone with her father
Is he still breathing?
No
I think I hear him breathing
No
He breathed so gently
No, he isn't breathing
But I think I feel a pulse!
No. It's your pulse you feel.

BEING SOMEWHERE DAVID BREEDEN

Come from somewhere
Angel of light
Don't we pray

Wind whistling the usual speed
Of change and nothingness

We do not make this up
We've been on the train
Racketing through various darknesses
Through various states

We have been far from home
And never remember leaving

Don't we pray
Angel of light
Come from somewhere

SEXT, FEBRUARY 25, 2007 DARREN J. N. MIDDLETON

Rise, my song, and have no fear
of soaring wide and high.
Christ the falconer is near,
Wherever you may fly.
 —"The Falconer," Richard Leach

All voices raised, the anthem sounds,
and every note gestures, lifts
upward, flyward, heavenward.
Today, though, Fedak's words unhinge, remove me.
Truth is, I thrum to Yeats, *his* falcon now mute. Likewise I,
wings fanned, stuck on the ground,
watching the reservations
rise,
moving
out
in
circles.

I pester God unremittingly.

JAPANESE PILGRIMAGE DARREN J. N. MIDDLETON

Witness to the strangulated prophesies
of ill-omened ravens astride vermillion-lacquered torri gates, he,

                                         in mid-life lost, would in vain
                             reach
for the purity of this place,
Kamakura, ancient city of samurai, west of heaven
and lonely without God. Only landscape
redeems,
her liturgy small comfort to his prayerless soul—
the fertile pines above Hakone,
Hiroshima's slate-grey sky, and the raked gravel of Ginkakuji temple. Landscape
redeems, takes his craven spirit and bids it sing.

    —Kyoto, Japan 2007

ON EARTH AMY LETTER

THE GARDEN BEHIND ANNA'S HOUSE grew green with shady trees and neat bright grass and wide inviting beds of flowers so thick I wanted to climb inside the softness and sweet smells and doze there forever in half-sleep. So many living, growing things asserted themselves there: snake tongues rose up from the earth like swords raised for battle, plush hibiscus opened wide in welcome, languidly weeping trees hung lines of flowers like fishing lures, and these would sway and beckon in the soft spring wind.

Anna stood with the pruning shears and a handful of flowers, a switch of an old woman ghastly white under her sun hat. I came to the gate and she welcomed me in. Babbling excitedly, I ran for the largest watering can.

A sun-blanched wooden fence protected this backyard paradise from the streetside and the neighbors, and at the back a path with steps led down to a sea wall covered with plants and climbing vines potted in the bellies of sailors, the backs of camels, the mouths of gators, and the baskets of fat laughing ladies, all shiny and brightly colored. In the center of the garden she kept an orange tree pruned at eye level, its fruit still small and green.

In my children's illustrated Bible, there was a picture of "Paradise on Earth": happy people of all races smiling together in a lush landscape where the lion and lamb both present themselves to be petted by children. Turn the people and animals into colorful ceramic pots, and it was Anna's garden.

She and I went to the same Kingdom Hall. On Saturdays we would go knocking door-to-door together. When we crossed streets, she held my hand. I loved Anna as a friend, and I sought her out often. When I was playing in the neighborhood, I would run to her fence, pull myself up, and look over. If she was there, I called her name until she unlatched the gate and let me in.

But this time, she stepped into the screened porch and put the flowers in a drinking glass. "It has to wait for Walter's dinner," she said. Anna's husband Walter was very ill, and I was too young to ask from what: he was sick, he had always been, and I did not question it. He lay in the bedroom down the hall, where the television flashed but made no sound.

While she cooked in the kitchen, I could talk to her from the back porch. I was too dirty to be allowed in, and inside it was too cold and dry for me to bear. I felt more comfortable in the heat, out among the wild things, the beetles, the blue jays, the lizards and frogs.

I saw a photo of parents and children framed upright beside the porch chair where Anna liked to sit. "Who's that?" I asked, like my mother would ask me gamely whenever the family photos came out.

"That's my daughter, Sylvia," Anna pointed with one wet finger, then scratched her nose and resumed washing the chicken livers. "Named for my mother. That's her husband Richard, and her grandson, James, her daughter Maria's first. James is in school now."

I looked at the baby in the picture and tried to imagine what he would look like, old enough to be in school, just a few years younger than me. Then I imagined Anna as my great-grandma. I had met my great-grandparents, the pair that was still living, but they lived far away, on a farm in Ohio, and spoke only Polish. Anna had an accent, but she could speak to me perfectly, and she lived only five houses away.

Anna put a skillet on the stovetop to heat and dried her hands. Her hands emerged from the sleeves of a thin flowery blouse, soft and impossibly white. On a table by the back patio door—beside the hand spade, the claw, the strange and wonderful attachments for the garden hose, the two big metal watering cans—Anna kept her garden gloves and wide-brimmed hats. All these sleeves and hats and gloves seemed very strange to me. I loved the feel of sun on my arms and rain in my hair, grass beneath my feet, bugs between my toes. My skin was browned, my fingers and toes scarred and dirty.

I had never thought of her as a great-grandmother before. I asked her how old she was. She didn't answer right away, so I said, "I'm almost eight years old."

She laughed. "I was born in 1902," she said. "I am so old, you, little girl, cannot understand how old. Or that I was born somewhere so far from here, this place did not exist when I was your . . . when I was even your parents' age."

She brought Walter's food to him on a tray, the tumbler of flowers next to the plate of livers, as though they were his drink. I waited on the porch, trying to picture Walter in my mind. I always pictured a man prone in bed, still as death, handsome, and not nearly as old as Anna. I pictured her slipping chicken livers and onions past his quiet lips. If I imagined him too long, his eyes would suddenly roll upward, spotting me watching him, accusing me . . . but Walter stayed at the end of the hall, in his room, and I never went there.

In the years that followed, I would often see Anna walking past my parents' house to go shopping or visit a neighbor. My family began attempting to celebrate Christmas: at first we just put lights on a potted palm, but within a couple of years it was a real pine tree, with lights and tinsel and a star. One December day I saw her walking past, and I became aware of the tree in the window, and I blushed red. I could tell she was averting her eyes from our house, careful not to see us. I wondered if she ever thought of me, and how she thought of me, and if she talked of me to Walter, and if Walter were alive or gone.

Anna returned from bringing Walter dinner. She put on her hat and gloves, and I followed her outside. I begged her to let me use the hose, and she consented. She fetched the metal watering can she'd left by the door. "Fill this up for me, good girl," she said.

I liked to watch the water bubble and gurgle in the confines of the can. The first spray of water made a tinny tapping, which lowered into a hollow sound that crept up in pitch until the can was full—it was like a tickle in my ear. Anna picked up the can and started down the steps to the sea wall. I directed the spray back towards the flowers.

"Don't forget the tongues," she said. Some people called them snake tongues or dragon tongues, and some called them mother-in-law tongues, but Anna just called them "tongues." She looked over her shoulder to make sure that I was watering them. She misplaced her foot and stumbled. Her arm caught against the steps, tearing her shirt. Blood spread out across her arm. I dropped the hose and ran to her.

"Shut off the hose," Anna said, taking off her gloves. "Don't flood the yard."

I turned the hose off. She scooped water from the can and patted it onto the scrape. Blood dripped onto the white cement. "A scrape is nothing to flood the yard for," she said.

"Are you okay?" was all I could say. She looked so small, crumpled there.

Anna forced a laugh. "You're so worried," she said. "You've never scraped yourself?"

I had, and I told her so. But it didn't seem to me like the same thing.

"This is nothing," she said. "But I liked this shirt." She looked at the torn shirt sleeve and sighed. She twisted her arm as though making sure the muscles still worked. That was when I saw the tattoo. It was almost the color of the veins visible through her skin, but too straight, and hazy, like the writing of a felt-tip pen on a napkin.

"What's that?" I said.

She was thoughtful for a moment. "A tattoo."

"What's it say?"

"It doesn't say anything." She splashed water to wash the blood off the cement. "They're numbers. Someone put it there long ago because they thought I was the wrong religion."

In my very limited way, I knew what it meant to be different: I had explained to disapproving teachers that I could not stand and say the pledge; I had been taunted by other children for celebrating neither Christmas nor Hanukkah. I thought I understood. "It's a tattoo for Jehovah's Witnesses," I said.

"No," she said. "Back then I was a Jew."

Now I was confused.

"We aren't all born Witnesses. Some of us became Witnesses later in life. When I was born, my parents were Jews, so I was a Jew."

"Are they still?" I asked, with such levels of optimism, I did not know.

"My parents died a long time ago. They were killed for being Jews."

"Killed," I said. "Who killed them?"

"Some good German citizen. Some patriot. It could have been anyone. Anyone, of course, but not a Witness. Witnesses would have nothing to do with it, and for that they were sent away with the Jews and the Gypsies and called traitors."

The canal in front of us was black and still. I could see Anna's reflection in it, but not my own. "If someone told me to kill somebody, I wouldn't do it. I wouldn't kill anyone," I said, to please her. I had no idea what I would do.

"I know you wouldn't. The bleeding's stopped. I'm going to dress it and change my shirt."

While Anna was inside, I finished watering the garden. The pinks and greens of the setting sun fell over the misted petals of all the flowers in the garden, and the world around me spun and glowed like a fevered, heated dream. I sprayed the water onto everything, all the beds, the bushes, the tongues, and the trees. When Anna returned, I was watering the small orange tree at the center of the garden. "Thank you," Anna said, taking the hose out of my hands. She turned it off and hung it from a limb of the low pruned tree. Her arm was bandaged with gauze, but she had not changed her shirt. She started to check the small green oranges that had only just begun to grow. "You'd better go home, now. It's dinner time."

IT WAS MORE THAN A MONTH before I saw Anna again, and everything had changed. My father decided to leave the church, and the Witnesses carry on the biblical tradition of casting out and stigmatizing those who are no longer part of the tribe. In some vague way I understood that there had been a change, that we no longer attended meetings two or three times a week, that my father was feeling pressure from all sides, that we were receiving unhappy visitors who had unpleasant things to say. But I had never associated any of this with Anna and her beautiful garden. Anna was a friend of mine, who loved me and let me help her water her yard. What could she have to do with decisions my parents made? What did she care about people who were angry with them?

I rang Anna's doorbell, and after a moment I saw her peek out from behind the blinds. She opened the door a crack. "You can't come here anymore," she said. "I'm sorry." She closed the door.

What she'd said made no sense to me. I rang the bell again, and again she opened the door. She only looked at me, her lips tight.

"Can I help water the garden?"

"No." She closed her eyes and sighed. "Tell your parents that you can't come back here until they've returned to us. What they're doing is wrong, very wrong. You need to tell them so. Now go home."

She closed the door. Slowly I walked to the end of the driveway, trying to understand why my friend turned me away. At the sidewalk I stopped and went back to Anna's door. I rang the doorbell again, and waited, but she did not answer. Finally, I went to the fence and pulled myself up to see. Anna stood with the hose in her hand, surrounded by mist and reflected light. I called out her name.

She turned towards me, angry. "Get down!" she said.

"I just want to help."

Anna unlatched the gate and I jumped down. "Don't you understand?" she said, as though I ought to. "If you want to come in, you have to tell your parents to go back to the Kingdom Hall and apologize."

"But you're my friend," I said.

"My friends are my brothers and sisters at the Kingdom Hall, and we will spend forever together. And if your parents do this, you won't be there. Now go home and tell your parents what I said, and do not come back until your family makes this right. Go."

She lifted her arm as though to close the gate but stopped when she saw me standing in its path. She turned her back. She walked away from me. She picked up the hose and continued watering. From where she watered, she ignored me completely. I was shunned.

I turned and faced the world. It was a poor suburb. The houses were old and weathered. Metal trash cans rolled back and forth in the curvature of concrete gutters. The sun seemed only to hang above Anna's backyard. Over the rest of the neighborhood, the sky was a mottled and forbidding indigo. Dogs barked behind chain-link fences. Some shirtless boys down the street, their bodies streaked with motor grease, revved the engine of a rusty truck, and laughed and shoved one another back and forth. I looked again at Anna's backyard, with its lusciously cultivated garden. The oranges were plumper than the last time I'd seen them but still green. The shade trees still dangled rows of flowers, tempting as lures. I took one last longing look at Anna, but she ignored me and made her way along the flower beds, still bright and soft with petals and shade, aiming the spray of water in an arc that misted and cast a rainbow in the air before her, the scaly green garden hose moving gently alongside her feet.

LOVE ANN IVERSON

Art is the only labour that succeeds by omission:
Between what we imagine and what's finally rendered
Is a world where only beautiful things that cannot exist are discovered.
  —Jude Nutter

But love, too, is another labor
that propels itself in oversight.
How often we see our ways of loving wrong—
Have I, do I, will I

loved, love you well enough?
Once I thought that love was a searching bird
flying in and out of my nest-like heart.
Or was it just a bird swooping to and from
my heart that had no likeness to its home?

In February the year after my father died
I painted twenty-three hearts
and sent them out like messenger pigeons.
Though I can rightly say I felt like I loved no one
which explains why none of them came back.

That was the year I thought of love
as a single tree without its leaves
in a blooming, ferocious jungle
that overlapped the boundaries
of what I've painted in my mind.
It stood there stark and useless
and I, a bird, looked on with shock and awe.

SUNFLOWERS ANN IVERSON

Sunflowers, Oil on Canvas, 1888
 —Vincent van Gogh

In sixth grade the teacher handed out a brochure from which to order prints of the classics for ninety-nine cents apiece. My mother ordered several, among them your *Sunflowers*, perhaps why we have these conversations.

Even in the print the impasto was quite evident and though just eleven years old, I thought the vase of the halfway-dying giants a bit peculiar, almost scary, like the tangling monsters in bad dreams. But their floppy, golden heads made her happy, and it made me happy to dutifully carry home to her a new print every month in its tubular container that we opened together on the kitchen table.

You painted them for Gauguin, who never made you happy, but the Sunflowers must have spoken to you of a life free of torment, one of complete elation. A life where yellow holds the brush and the eyes of life and death are equal in their beauty.

And Gauguin painted you painting them as though the two of you followed in a circle those nine autumn weeks in and out of the yellow house in Arles until the tragic took the canvas over.

I remember them in the living room in their great oak frame she bought at the Salvation Army, then again in the kitchen, and then again in the hall, over her bed, and then back again to the living room. Oh, she moved your flowers around so much, and all I did was follow them around
and her.

AFTER PAINTING ANN IVERSON

Red is making love
and yellow stands for birth.
Plum is the color of a baby.

Turquoise is that old idea,
the lip of a can on the shelf,
just waiting to say it all over again.

Green is an argument
and consequently blue
after it's been washed over
in my mind for all these years.

SOLSTICE NEARING ANN IVERSON

If you could see the sun as I do every morning stepping the horizon, not missing a rung, its generous offering of saturated orange beyond belonging or the obligatory.

If you could see the crescent moon as I do, both of us quiet and dark in the undulating night knowing it won't always be like this. The moon will stay the same, only turning its face from side to side, but will never leave the orbit, as you and I will, have to, and will.

Whichever way I'm going, I take the long way, same road winding and curving through the trees like the soul hovering over the place of death then finally spinning off into the contractual light that we call God.

People exist only in their minds and sense of duty until the hint of the afterworld appears slight, unjust, promising and there. When there are so many *ifs* too much can happen.

If the heart is strong enough.
If the moon is wise.
If heaven has a place.

THE PEGASUS LANDING ZACHARY DAVIS

'Jack stood behind the house where his grass met with gravel from the quarry. It was early morning and the air was bitter from cold and the pungent smell of the mill on the other side of town. Early rains had brought a few feet of dark water to the bottom of the quarry; a stream flowed off on the far side where the tractors and trucks had come and gone throughout the summer.

There was an agitation in the air followed by fluttering as a few dozen geese took flight off the water. As they passed out of the hole, Jack followed their upward motion and watched as they disappeared over the top of his house. Tomorrow others would come and replace those that left.

Elle was at the table with a coffee mug when Jack entered the house. Her thin knees were collected and the end of her little nightgown was pulled tight down to her feet.

—I dreamed that I grew a pair of wings, Jack said as he poured coffee into his mug.

Elle held her mug with both hands close together and her mouth was right over the lip. She was looking out the screen at where her husband had just been standing.

—Big ol' angel wings. Can't think of the last time a dream felt so real, he said. Jack pulled back a chair and sat down.

Elle swallowed coffee.

—You mind getting breakfast on your way? The eggs are bad.

—That's fine.

—Have you ever had that dream before?

—Never.

—Was I in it?

—Nuh-uh. It was just me. I was out in a field and the Ford wouldn't start and then I noticed that I had these wings on my back.

—Did you fly?

—Didn't know how. I just stood there. Couldn't start the Ford and couldn't fly worth a damn. But I could sorta see myself from a distance, and it was a good-looking picture of me and my wings next to the truck in that field.

—That's nice, but ya shoulda tried to fly.

—Didn't work like that.

Jack went into the living room and pulled on his jacket.

—Bye.

Jack stopped at a restaurant and ordered a coffee and pancakes. He read half of the article on the front page of the daily and paid at the counter.

In the parking lot three Hispanics stood out by the road waiting to be picked up. As Jack pulled out onto the road a van came up and two of the Hispanics jumped into the back. The other fellow stayed standing as the van left and, as it distanced, the remaining Hispanic squatted down on his haunches and lit a cigarette.

Jack turned down the radio as he drove the Ford up to the booth at the entrance to the mill. Caleb worked the booth and slid open the window as Jack pulled up.

—Morning, said Jack.

—Where'd you sleep last night?

—What?

—Elle has called three times asking for ya.

—What did she say?

—Just needs you to call her.

—I was eatin' breakfast. Mind if I use your phone?

—Sure.

Jack pulled out of the lane and parked the truck. Inside the tiny booth Jack dialed home as another couple of guys came through and clocked in. Elle answered and was upset.

—What's the matter?

—After you left I went outside and I found a dead horse by the side of the house.

—A horse?

—Right on the side.

—Are you sure it's dead?

—Pretty sure.

—It must of wandered over from Deassey's and been sick.

—I don't think so. It looks like someone killed 'im. I want you to come home and see it. Jack, it scares me.

—Alright. I will be right there. Caleb, clock me back out. I need to run home.

—Sure Jack. Everything all right?
—Yeah everything is fine. Elle says there's a horse got killed in our yard.
—Well hell. Probably is from Deassey's.
—I know it. I'll call him when I get home. Try to be back soon.
—Yeah fine.

Elle was standing out on the driveway when Jack pulled in. She was wearing his long coat and a pair of rubber boots.
—It's over here.

He followed her around the house to where a black speckled horse lay on its side in the long grass. She stopped a few feet from it.
—Go look at his head.

Jack walked up and pulled back some grass to expose the horse's head. The top of the animal's skull had been crushed in from up between the ears down to the animal's eyes. All four legs were crumpled under the body and looked broken at several places. The grass was covered in blood and matter. Blood was in the nose and the horse's tongue lay limp out of his mouth.
—Jesus.
—I know it. It's horrible.
—I need to call Deassey, see if he's missing this.
—I think this is some kind of crime. You should call the sheriff.
—Maybe. I'm going to call Deassey first.

When Jack hung up the phone, Elle had dressed and was holding her bag in the living room.
—What did he say?
—He went and checked and isn't missing any of his horses.
—Where did that come from then?
—No idea.
—Call the sheriff. I need to go.
—Alright.

Jack walked her out to her car and when Elle had gone, he went back around and stood over the horse. He looked at the grass; there were no signs of tire tracks or trampled areas from someone dragging the animal.
—Thing didn't fall from the sky.

The horse didn't give any answers; his tongue lay limp.

It had started raining by the time Jack went inside and called the sheriff's office.
—This is Jack Wyeth. Someone dumped a dead horse on my property.

The sheriff's secretary asked if the horse belonged to Jack.

—No, we don't have any livestock. We just found it this morning. But it was beat pretty bad, and I would like the sheriff to come down and take a look.

The secretary didn't say anything as she was typing. Finally she said that the sheriff would be right over.

Jack watched from the front window and soon the sheriff's truck pulled into the driveway. Jack walked out towards the truck as Sheriff Laurel stepped out wearing a big green rain slicker.

—What have you got, Wyeth?

The two men shook hands.

—Thanks for coming down. Elle found this out on the side after I left for work, said Jack as he led Laurel around the side to where the horse lay.

—How is Elle?

—She's fine. Started working at the pharmacist's about a month ago. She likes it.

—Well Christ, said Laurel as he looked down at the horse. At least the rain is keeping the flies off and the smell down. But Christ.

Laurel stepped carefully around the big animal and lifted up one of his legs to see underneath. He scanned the area around the horse.

—Did you move it at all?

—No. All I did was pull back the grass around it to get a better look. When I came out this morning I swear there wasn't any grass bothered and no footprints.

The sheriff looked back at the area of the grass that they had trampled moments before. The rain and muddy ground left big imprints of where the two men had just walked.

—That's strange, Wyeth. You sure this wasn't here yesterday?

—Positive. I came out here to the side last night to get firewood. I woulda seen it.

—Well, it rained most of the night and I don't understand how this got here. There aren't any footprints or tire tracks and this horse woulda been heavy as hell. I assume that somebody was meaning to dump it in the quarry and only got this far. You hear anything?

—No. I am usually a light sleeper but I slept like a baby last night.

—I don't get it. You call Deassey or Hardy?

—I called Deassey.

—I'll give Hardy a call when I get back to the office. If I don't get anything I'll get a couple of guys to come down and load this in the truck.

—Sounds good. Thanks.

Jack and Laurel turned and walked back around the house to the truck.

—Sheriff, any news from your daughter?

—Not for a couple of weeks. I'm sure she is doing just fine. But I'll tell you, it makes ya ask what the hell it is we've done here.

The sheriff stepped up into the cab of his truck.

—And been talking to God a little more regularly.

Jack nodded.

—Give Elle my regards. And I will call Hardy.

—Thanks.

The truck pulled out and down the road and Jack walked back inside.

Jack took his sandwich out of the fridge and returned it to his lunch pail. He filled his thermos with the coffee that was left in the pot and walked out of the house.

He went across the lawn to his truck and put his lunch and thermos on the passenger seat. Jack sat for a moment idling with the radio on and then turned off the truck and opened the glove box. He pulled out a couple of oil rags and, taking them, got out.

He walked back inside and went into the bathroom. In the cabinet he pulled out a big jug of rubbing alcohol. Elle's toothbrush and paste were on the sink so Jack screwed on the cap and put them away. He peed and shut the door behind him.

—This is Jack. I had the sheriff here and will be another hour.

At the mill Caleb said that Jack could take his time and it was fine. Jack thanked Caleb and hung up the phone.

Out in the tall grass, Jack stood over the horse. He poured the alcohol over one of the rags and dabbed at the crusted blood around the animal's nostrils. He gently wiped it away and poured more alcohol onto the rag. Then he went to work on the gaping, crushed skull, wiping up the bits of matter around the head and tenderly cleaned around the dark eye.

—Dreaming that I had grew wings while you were being beat all to hell.

As Jack apologized he dropped the first rag onto the grass and took the other one from his side, pouring on the alcohol, he rubbed down the matte until the horse's fur was clean and glossy.

He straightened the broken legs and stood back and appraised his work.

The animal was quiet except for the soft drumming of rain on its big belly.

Jack pulled a blue tarp from the shed and covered the horse and then washed his hands at the faucet on the side of the house. He went and locked the front door of the house and then started the Ford and drove towards the mill.

Jack finished his shift and was home before Elle. The horse was gone and Jack's tarp was folded by the driveway. He drank a beer inside and called the sheriff's office.

The horse had been boarding at Hardy's, owned by the wife of a rich fellow from Royal. The sheriff said that Hardy didn't know how any of it happened and added that he still couldn't figure how the horse could have ended up in the Wyeths' yard.

—Can't say not knowing.

When Elle got home she made dinner and they ate in front of the TV. After dinner Jack changed the Ford's oil in the garage and then showered before going into the bedroom. Elle was already under the covers when Jack sat down on the side of the bed.

—You asleep?

—No.

—Laurel said hello.

—I like him. You know they haven't heard from their daughter in a while.

—He said that today.

—They're good people.

Jack was silent. He was looking out the window. It was dark. Just beyond the reach of the light on the back porch lay the quarry—that immense, dark pit.

—I keep thinking about that poor horse, said Elle.

—Yeah.

—What kind of a person would do that?

—I don't know.

She shuddered and pulled the comforter farther up.

Jack turned off the porch lights and checked the locks on the doors. He pulled back the covers and slipped into bed and lay there on his back looking up at the ceiling. The only sound was Elle's breathing and the sound of rain. After a few moments Jack got up out of bed and walked out of the room. He went into the living room and turned the porch lights back on. He got back into bed.

—What did you just do?

—Turned on the porch lights.

Jack watched as a gust of wind pushed rain against the window.

WALKING BACK TO THE FERRY, BÜYÜKADA   JENNIFER G. STEWART

In fairy tales
men and gods assume the form
of swans and fish, of snakes that slip in pockets,
of crows entangling in some dryad's hair.
They're harmless frogs at the water-well,
waiting to be princes.
Or in fiercer tales, they're dragons
who must conceal their scales from maidens,
giants waiting to be woken from beneath
blankets of tall hills.
Benevolent trees and evil waters,
gods of wind-wave and night-drape.

Which of you was it, then,
who matched our quickened steps
through the forest in the twilight?
Flanking our thin shadows
behind and beside,
as the sun left the cooling sky
and draped the sleeping island forms
with dread?

Your brown heads, tongues wagging,
an escort of mutts
brought us back to town.
Whose messengers were you?
What our watchers' names?

ALL SAINTS' DAY, ISTANBUL JENNIFER G. STEWART

Morning in pajamas
speaking of the saints—
how their questions could not have been
heavier than ours,

I think of Saint Teresa,
hands splayed in transfiguration.
Julian in her cell.
Saint Francis on the hillside
letting the birds go free.
Saint Lucia blinded
by numinous light.

When the prayer call rends
the rain-soaked air,

decision.

We bend necks,
cup hands.
Trying to catch
what it is
they must have known.

AMERICAN DREAM JUSTIN RYAN BOYER

Together, the sun and moon fear
what we've become; too close to place,
but seen as we stand in the driveway
staring down the block—years gone.
Copies of a copy are the houses
all dressed up for the masquerade. Dream

seldom, sleep often. Mama cries her dream
to sleep and shares her fear
with smiles delivered to neighborhood houses.
Dad never tucks us in and this place
drove away sister, now so far gone.
"Don't tell," she said, walking off the driveway

at 2 a.m. I lay on the cracked driveway
and wait for mourning to bring a dream
of relief. We sold the trailer and, gone
with it, my sincerity. I breathe with a fear
that won't admit I feel out of place.
Five bedrooms, three vacant: one houses

a naked, antique vanity—the other houses
barrenness with hope. The street-lit driveway
is my undisclosed haven, my midnight place
of refuge and prayer. Peering up into God's dream
I take fruit from the tree of life—be still—and push fear
away for a moment until forgotten and again gone

is my sanity. Now if there is anything gone
worth more than envy and straw houses,

AMERICAN DREAM

please remind my ragged soul. Because fear,
in the open, finds an edge in the driveway
that cuts just to see the color of a dream
escape its confinements and move into a place

where it can be free from expectations. Place
your hands on me Mama. I know you were gone
long before sister left our imprisoned dream.
We're trapped in the night; we built houses
and mistook them for peace. The driveway
is filled with hearses, our checkbooks with fear.

Life has left this place. Emptiness houses
our souls, which are now gone, parked in the driveway,
toasting the American Dream—living in fear.

FACES SHELLY DRANCIK

Hours ago (or was it days), the whiskey scorched then soothed his aged throat. His blood thawed, if for a moment.

He sees their faces when the sun ascends above the lake and again when the sun escapes the concrete walls. They block their faces from the cold, from the wind, from him.

His stomach twists, aches for food, begs for it. Corroded fingers grip his white cup. Two silver coins and a pool of copper. Today, he tells himself, I will eat.

But whiskey would warm his body.

More glances—mostly glares—come his way. Eyes always speak. A bus passes, coats him with smell and slime. He should move his camp.

A woman wearing a long camel-hair coat pauses in front of him. A wool scarf warms her face, covers her smile. She looks at his feet; he wears one white sneaker and one black loafer. The smooth of her leather glove reaches his threadbare palm.

God bless you, he says, and means it. The woman walks into the curl of the wind.

A bar of chocolate wrapped in golden paper. He feels the thick edges, weight like a pound of gold. Presses it to his weathered cheek and breathes dark cocoa through the golden paper.

He was four, maybe five. A Sunday morning with iced-blue skies. His mom and sister stayed home with the flu. In the wooden pew, he sat close to his father, fighting the fidgets that inched up his body. He stood when his father stood, sat when he sat. Followed him to his knees. Afterwards, his father took him to Lou's on the corner to buy him a chocolate bar; he devoured it in a few bites. Slow down, partner, his father laughed.

He strokes the glossy words on the golden paper. They speak of a distant country; the country that absorbed his father's blood in battle, in the second of world wars.

Soon after the knock on their apartment door, madness rocked his mother in her wooden chair. An aunt in Indiana asked to keep his sister. Shuffled from home to home, misery became his mother.

He tears the golden paper. The surge of cocoa overwhelms his tongue, burns his throat. *Slow down, partner, his father says.* Wind dies down. Cold hides behind the buildings.
Faces pass by.

DAFFODILS LARRY D. THOMAS

With each percussive wave of clappers
clanging against the lips of bells,

they shudder in first light
and they reel in the churchyard,

brushed by the habits of flowing nuns
rushing to Mass. They shudder

in first light, irreverent with yellow,
these florid genitalia

of diminutive plants
flaunting their little crimes

of public lewdness, brandishing
their petals like brazen pirates.

HE CLOTHES THEM LARRY D. THOMAS

for R.C. Gorman

with fields
of pure color.
They flow,

these women
of the Taos
Pueblo,

even
as they sit
on holy

desert ground.
He knows
the power

of the flesh,
ever true
to his vow

to render it
sacred,
shrouding it

with the purity
of hue,
exposing it

LARRY D. THOMAS

    only
    in their brown,
    hallowed feet

    and the sure,
    muscular grace
    of their hands.

IN SIN SO CRAFTILY MORTAL LARRY D. THOMAS

On delicate leaves
reddened with the flush of birth,

the late March sun
lays its hands of fire

where jays ablaze with blue
are thrashing, hubristic

in the sophistry of squawking,
cobalt Lucifers

so rabid with the blood of life
that holiest water

flung across their backs
in a rite of cloudburst-exorcism

musses nary a feather
of their arrogance.

DAYLIGHT SAVINGS ED HIGGINS

all this breakage   of time
       backwards &
                    forwards   every fall & spring

it's hardly a sigh you'll say
       in the breadth or breath of larger things

but
I wonder   about absolutes   shifted
    here   then   later   there

I'm nervous
    for instance   that my front yard maple

must ripen   to ecstasy   on autumn's
             red
             yellow
             and
             burnt amber
leaf-time
       or later when the lavender crocus
& May   everywhere
must be about   the undoing   of winter
    into   those new grey-greens

or do the dead   I wonder   ever know
    we play such   tricks   on them

turning over   time   then back again

       these equivocal hours   they
no longer can calculate

and what errors   must fret   the distant stars
in their   long   journey

alighting now   upon   earth's
                                 uncertain

time.

WHEN I WAS TWELVE STACY BARTON

IT WAS THE SUMMER I TURNED TWELVE that I heard the voice of God. It was also the summer my pappy died and NASA put a man on the moon. Everything about that summer was strange. I remember it like a movie. It started out ordinary enough; we still had our farm outside Pensacola and the days were hot and humid like always—one right after the other—but once Apollo landed on the moon, everything changed.

That Monday night us kids sat on the floor, glued to the flicker of black and white as Neil Armstrong took one giant step for mankind. We cheered, Mamma put her hands over her face, and Pappy leaned back, all emotional. He said he was glad no one had proclaimed—like those horrible Russians had—that there was no God in heaven. It was the only time I ever saw him cry.

The next day Mamma was folding the sheets off the line, Pappy was coming in off the tractor and Tommy and I were playing under the porch. The afternoon was mostly quiet, one of those days when the air hangs limp beside you. Sarah and little May were playing inside with their girl things and Tommy and I were stalking whatever wild creature we hoped we might find under the floorboards.

Pappy strode across the yard and right up the steps of the porch and when his boot hit that third step I heard, "Jesse," in the creak of the board. But it sounded like this, "Jesseee." Suddenly I was in the belly of a whale all boarded up in the soft sand and darkness. I blinked and looked through the cracks of light making zebra stripes across Tommy's face and said, "You hear that?"

"What?" he said, his left eye eager in a beam of light.

"I'm not sure."

"Well, what'd it sound like?"

"Well . . . God . . . I guess," I said, a little afraid.

"Reckon I did not," Tommy said and spit. I could see he was disappointed; he hoped I'd heard the neighbor's cat.

Tommy didn't share my fascination with the divine. He didn't even like Sunday school. He wasn't big on believing anything, really—except that he would walk on the moon someday. Tommy wanted to be an astronaut; he had his sights set on the Cape. I wanted to be a preacher, and Pensacola suited me just fine. When no one was looking I made the back of Pappy's chair a pulpit and rocked from heel to toe and back again, practicing my holy moves. One time I actually felt like maybe the Holy Spirit was atop my head in a lick of fire, but I never told anyone.

Over fried ham and snap beans on Wednesday I asked Pappy if he had ever heard from God. He raised his eyebrows and looked at me. Mamma and the girls stopped talking. Tommy snorted.

"You mean out loud?" Pappy asked.

"Yes sir, like Samuel in the Bible."

"Well, no, Jesse," he said, considering me carefully. "I don't believe I have."

I asked Sarah to pass the butter, and I spread it too thick on my biscuit while I waited for everyone to forget what I had said. Sometimes I wished I didn't believe.

By Friday night I lay in bed in my room with Tommy, still wondering what it was that I had heard under the porch. It could have been the voice of God. That wasn't any harder to believe than a man walking on the moon.

The window lace hung still in the August heat. Sarah and little May were already asleep across the hall—all of us spread on top of our summer covers. I listened hard to see if I could hear the voice again, but all I heard were tree frogs and cicadas making noise outside my window. No God. No breeze either. From where I was I couldn't even see the moon. But it spilled into our room through the oak tree and made shapes on the floorboards that seemed to move under the hand of God. I wondered if we moved under the hand of God, too.

I saw a light under our door, so I slipped out of bed and peeked through the crack into the other room. There he was, on his knees beside the chair, the Bible spread before him. It was strange to see my father that way, bowing his head into the hands that could do anything: fix a tractor, plow a field, build a shelf for Mamma. The air was holy somehow in the small circle of light that surrounded him and I was glad I had my shoes off. I shut the door softly and went back to bed. I lay on my back with my arms behind my head and looked up at the ceiling. After awhile I closed my eyes and made myself like Pappy, like Samuel in the Bible, listening for God to call my name.

"Jesse!" Pappy called from the barn the next morning.

"Yes sir?" I hollered back.

"Mind you look out for Sarah and little May, and don't let Thomas get into trouble!"

"Yes sir!"

Saturdays Pappy let us have the whole day to ourselves, no chores. This Saturday—like almost all of them—we were going swimming! We walked the sandy road past the Turners' place, around the back side, until we came out near the lake. One big old oak, hung thick with Spanish moss, made a cave of shade all the way down to the water. It was quiet and leaf-crunchy, musty and fresh, all at the same time.

"Tag!" Tommy said, slapping Sarah on the back and running. "You're it!"

"No fair!" she hollered and ran after him.

Little May squealed and jumped up and down in the same spot and went nowhere.

"Come on, May," I said, laughing, and took her hand.

Tommy stripped down and jumped in first, then Sarah, then May, and finally me. Our clothes littered the bank like pictures from the Sears catalog. The water was cool, the air was warm; I dove to the bottom to see if I could find an arrowhead.

The world above melted into the quiet underneath. It pressed into my ears and cooled my face. Upside down, I dug my hands into the sand, feeling for anything sharp and smooth and pointed. Just then, I heard a sound rolling and tumbling toward me.

"Jesseee."

I nearly inhaled a lungful of water, spun, and kicked to the surface as fast as I could. I came up coughing and spitting. "What was that?" I said, paddling around.

The others stopped splashing and looked over at me. Sarah said, "What?"

They hadn't heard it.

I turned away and shouted, "What?" I swam in circles and looked around at the bank. "I'm here!" I hollered. Then I listened, hard, but all I heard were Sarah and Tommy and little May paddling around beside me. No one else was there, only trees and lake water and an old trailing vine sweeping silently down the bank.

May looked on, her eyes wide and still.

Tommy was irritated; he wanted to get back to his game. "Who you talking to?" he said, smirking. "God?"

"I dunno," I said and swam away; I felt funny.

Our fingers and toes were pale little raisins by the time the storm came. It was one of those summer storms that brews out over the Gulf and brings a breeze by supper. It hadn't rained enough the past few weeks and just that morning Pappy had worried that everything was "kindlin' dry."

We laughed on the water as the storm came and watched it sprawl across the sky. It was dark and full of itself and we raced it all the way home, big pellets of rain urging us on. By the time we made it to the house, the rain was pounding white and hard and we were wetter than we'd been in the lake. Mamma brought towels and all of us sat out on the porch while it poured. We ate Mamma's brown beans from warm bowls and smelled the wet earth and the just-washed stone. The porch tin bounced and the thunder cracked and we stuck our heads under the busted gutter and laughed.

But what started as a simple shower soon changed. The thundercloud we'd raced all the way home became a horrible house of lightning; it struck a flare so loud and blue that even Mamma started. It wasn't long after that Mrs. Turner came running, clutching her yellow cat, sobbing about the old oak tree.

"It split in the storm and burst itself into fire!" she wailed. The cat squirmed in her arms and her eyes spread wide at Pappy. "Ned's trying to save the house."

The cat jumped down like an exclamation point and Pappy ran. Mamma brought Mrs. Turner in, without the cat, and we all sat quiet while that fire ate everything the Turners owned and Pappy saved Ned from doing something foolish.

Eventually a cloud of smoke came our way, headed down the road towards us from the Turners'. Mamma and Mrs. Turner held each other at the window and repeated, "Please God no . . . please, God no," as we watched it crash through the brush like a dragon. The fire flew, full of meanness now, out to take our barn next for sure. Pappy fought it though, and Ned with him. Mamma made us hide under the bed with wet kerchiefs on our noses while she and Mrs. Turner went out to help the men. After awhile I pushed Tommy out and said, "Let's go!"

He nodded and we wiggled around the girls.

"Keep little May close," I said as stern as I could to Sarah.

By the time we got outside, the ladder truck was there and lots of other men; it was loud and wild, with Fourth of July sparks and a bright orange thrill. The air felt wet and tasted sour. The men hollered in the haze and threw big hoses from one to another and carted around sloppy wet sacks. I grabbed Tommy's arm and pointed across the property; Pappy had already saved the tractor. Tommy nodded and we looked for Pappy, but we couldn't find him in the uproar. Then we crouched on the porch step to keep from being seen and felt the danger in the heat of the fire when the wind blew.

Everyone worked to save the barn until the last, and it wasn't until later, when Mrs. Turner let Sarah and May out from under the bed that we knew what we had lost. It wasn't the tractor; Pappy had bravely saved that. And the barn had burned, but not past repair, thanks to the ladder truck and the men. Mrs. Turner told us they were bandaging Mamma's hands where she had scorched them slapping back sparks, but she'd be all right. And Ned said that even though some cinders singed the house, it had survived.

"But where's Pappy?"

Ned cleared his throat when we asked, pressed his lips together once and said, "Well, he got the smoke in him."

"But he's okay?" Sarah asked.

"Shoot, he's Pappy, stupid, he's fine. Right?" Tommy laughed but everyone else was quiet. I felt the air fade away. Mrs. Turner pulled little May onto her lap and looked at Ned.

"He filled his lungs too full of smoke trying to save everything for you kids and your Mamma," Ned said. His voice wavered and he looked at me; his eyes were red behind a face smeared with smoke.

"Yeah but he's . . . he's not hurt too bad, right?" I asked. The fear of those words choked my eyes worse than the smoke.

"I'm afraid he was, children," Ned said gently. "Truth is . . . he's gone."

We stood there a minute, nobody saying anything. It was like being under water and unable to come up. Little May started to whimper. I heard the men call to one another in the yard; Pappy's voice was not among them. It didn't seem possible.

Tommy punched Ned as hard as he could in the stomach. "You're lying!" he hollered. He leapt off the porch and ran flailing toward the barn shouting, "Pappy!"

Ned looked at me and I knew I was the one who had to run after Tommy. I caught up with him at the back of the ladder truck. Mamma was there, with Pappy's sooty head pulled sideways in her lap; he didn't look like himself at all. Mamma barely knew we were there.

Tommy slid behind me and I stepped closer. I touched Pappy's forehead; it was cold. He didn't move. He didn't speak. He didn't pray. Neither did I. Not until Ned came and pulled us both away did I realize I was crying.

Mrs. Turner saw we got something warm to eat—Mamma's brown beans were a memory of another life by then—and Ned fixed a spot in the barn for the animals. Mamma had gone with the men to take Pappy into Pensacola and so I helped Tommy and Sarah and little May wash up and climb into bed. Even with soap we were all so tacky black that Mamma would have to wash our sheets again.

It was hard to sleep and hard to stay awake; I paced between the beds.

"I want Mommy," little May whimpered.

I patted her back and smoothed her hair, like Mamma did.

"We gonna be alright?" Sarah whispered.

"Of course," I answered.

Sarah leaned back on her pillow. I went on, "Bet you a nickel Mamma makes us sausage and eggs tomorrow. Maybe even some buttermilk." Of course I had no idea if Mamma would even be back by morning, but it was something to say.

"Who's gonna milk the cows?" Tommy called from across the hall. He said it too loudly and I could tell he was scared. He was thinking about Pappy. We were all thinking about Pappy, or rather we were all thinking about how he wasn't there.

No one said anything else after that, and when it got quiet May curled up against Sarah and went to sleep. After awhile Tommy stretched out with his arms behind his head. Pretty soon I heard Sarah's breath, and Tommy's, going in and out with May's.

I stood alone in the hall, bare feet on the floorboards, and half hoped the voice would come, but the night was quiet; even the tree frogs and cicadas were silenced by the fire. I walked to the front of the house, to the corner where my father prayed. The smell of new ashes came in the open window and clung to everything and I wondered if I had ever heard from God or if it even mattered now.

Our Father who art in heaven, hallowed be thy name . . . I knelt beside the window, its wooden sill sticky and cool beneath my arms. It was hard to breathe. I looked up at the sky that had held a man on the moon—God hadn't been there. I dug my chin into the back of my hand; I was not going to cry. I glared at the broken barn, the tractor in the yard, and the place where my father should have been. God hadn't been in the fire either. An ache sat like straw in my belly. I kept it there as long as I could, but as the night settled into sleep, the straw turned into tears; I gripped the sill while they shook me without sound.

It was then that the voice streamed in the window like the Pentecost and blew back my hair. The sound of it was deep and sad and long, as though God himself was crying my name. I was afraid it would wake the others, and more afraid that it would not.

I don't know how long I knelt there, but at some point little May started crying and the spell was broken. I stood up to go to her and noticed the moon—it had risen fully by then and flooded the yard with light. It was beautiful. In that one moment by the window, before I went to comfort May, I hated God for taking my Pappy, but I knew the Russians were wrong.

GRACE AMANDA MCQUADE

When I was three they left me,
My family, in one of those pits
That children play in—
Up to my neck in plastic balls.

My little arms cupped each one,
Turning over yellow, green
And following that rough seam
Around their centers.

And I waited, unaware
That I was lost at all.
My brown hair curled
On the bottoms, bouncing

With every jump I took
Back into the sea of dots,
Thinking I might be some fish
Misplaced—out of water,

Thirsty, hot, sweaty, yet
Content to play—lonely
As other kids came and went,
Their parents looking madly,

While on the pavement treaded
My only relatives, frantically
Searching for me, alone
In my own captivity.

STORY OF A TREE ELIZA KELLEY

She did not know that it was I who gave her the grain, the wine, and the oil, and who lavished upon her silver and gold that they used for ba'al.
    —Hosea 2:8

Since the road took me north
you remain
among jonquil bulbs—the last thing I recall
after you drove away, and I
just stood there, looking
down, the way people do
who can't think up any excuse
for whatever
lies unspoken, even now.

How does it happen, that
old bulbs always manage to answer
at precisely the hardest moment, looking up
through Virginia cast-iron
February ground, licking
flurries splattered
on shadow-damp straw mulch, magnolia
buds hovering above
such a careful brown
boulevard garden, unaware of the sad
darkening of that sudden almost
into this dead graphite
rock salt snow?

It is the way of curbs, I suppose,
to hold back the flood or accept the weight

STORY OF A TREE

of each unwanted storm in turn, the worst
completely toppling
twenty-year-old flowering Valentine sprigs
grown into this uprooted Jesse Tree, wind-stripped
naked except for the heaviest limbs, sharply bereft
of past promises.

There is always one broken thing we most wish
back, that is furthest lost, the absence
embraced by its own present, the almost
touchable warmth we try to remember, something
we could not say—
at least once
we knew what it was, and still
we call it the word some of us
are not allowed.

LETTERS HOME FROM SUNSHINE MOUNTAIN JILL NOEL KANDEL

God had a wonderful plan for your life that went like this: become a nurse, marry foreign, move away, and serve. Third world here you come. It had sounded nice in Sunday school when you were a girl—a good girl, a chin-up, cheer-up, sit-in-the-front-row girl. After your first year of perfect attendance you received a circular golden brooch with leaves embossed around it like an Olympic medal. Your teacher pinned it on and the class sang *Climb, climb up Sunshine Mountain faces all aglow.* Each year a perfect attendance bar was added. By the age of twelve your sweater was covered with medals, like a veteran of foreign wars.

You married and moved overseas where the poverty and hunger you'd read about became part of your life; the pages turned slowly year after year. So what were you supposed to think when the wonderful plan wasn't so wonderful? Either God had botched it, or you had. It was a difficult call. You didn't want to look the buffoon. God didn't either.

So you backpedaled into the light of Sunshine Mountain—your safe and happy haven—and picked up your pen. You drew a permanent grin on your face and wrote cheerful letters home.

Government Republic of Zambia, 1983

Dear Mom and Dad,

It's a funny thing. Can you imagine? I haven't gotten any mail for a month. I went to the post office to ask what's going on and found out that all of our post—as they say in Zambian-British-English—is sitting at the Mongu office waiting for the airplane to bring it here.

Johan says the Zambian government hasn't paid the carrier for a few months and they are refusing to fly into Kalabo until they're paid. It might be awhile.

Since we've been given a government house to live in it is the government who takes care of paint. When we moved in every room was either dark navy blue or black. It was rather depressing to say nothing about dingy and dirty. Two weeks ago the Government Republic of Zambia sent over a couple painters. They came with one brush and a dented can of watered down white paint. It took four hours to paint half of a wall! The paint was so thin I could see through it.

It has taken two weeks to get one wall painted. I am so frustrated with it that all I can do is laugh. It isn't even funny. But I just keep laughing. It relieves the tension but leaves me with a terrific headache.

If nothing else life in Zambia is quite unpredictable.

Love,

Jill

YOU HID YOURSELF BEHIND THIN BLUE AEROGRAMMES decked with magnificent Zambian stamps. Your mother kept every one you sent her. Shoeboxes full of them stuffed into a small cupboard. They are upbeat letters full of anecdotal stories: the robberies, cobras, and black mamba snakes. The African Fish Eagles, Blue Headed Agamas, and squeaky sand. Cooking pumpkin leaves, eating radish soup. The children's births, their first words, first steps, and first teeth.

All those pieces of paper, folded and stored away, are full of blue ink particulars that perpetuate fiction: splendid agricultural development work, happy housewife, exotic Africa. When you go back and read them now, it is as if you are reading something a stranger wrote. Your letters and your memories testify to two separate lives. You wrote home in words conceived through eyes of wonder that gazed out at a world so different all you could do was sit down and record the parade. You mailed off those cheerful letters, and then late at night you cried yourself to sleep.

You came back from Africa years later full of sand and dirt and didn't talk about it because no one wanted to hear. Your Christian friends least of all. They liked victorious stories. They liked to hear the happy-ever-after endings, full of angel wings and rapture.

You didn't talk about your story. Not the first pages. Not the first years. But then, you were just like your friends. You, too, wanted only a Lazarus story: after the tomb. Not the decay. You wanted a Job story, at the end that is, number of children doubled, camels too. Forget about the wife. You didn't want the ash heap, dripping blisters, head between your hands. But that is what you got. You wondered why you ever went. Had it been a mistake? If so, was it yours . . . or God's?

Dear Mom and Dad,

It's been three months. No mail in sight. Isn't it funny?

I'm very busy these days. We had "company" staying at our house thirteen of the thirty days in June. There isn't a hotel in our village so every expatriate, embassy worker, or United Nations employee on a mission seems to come knocking at our door. Mostly we get agriculture guys coming to talk to Johan about his work. Pretty soon I'll know as much about wheat and rice as Johan does. It seems the only thing anybody wants to talk about.

We've had a few hippie types just passing through.

They say, "Africa is quite an experience."

I want to say, "I wish you'd wash your own dishes." But I don't. You taught me too well. I am polite.

I keep busy. I never knew how much work a washing machine, dryer, dishwasher, fridge, freezer, and vacuum saved me! The hardest thing is trying to find enough food to feed all these people. What do they think? It grows on trees? Ha-ha.

Love and miss you,

Jill

THERE WERE FOUR WAYS TO LEAVE KALABO. You tried them all. You sat in a banana boat with plank seating, eight to twelve hours to the next town. The children in the boat couldn't wait that long to pee. Their parents held them hanging over the side of the canoe as they peed into the mighty Zambezi River. You watched, gripping little babies in your mind, hold them tight mom. Don't let them fall. You dreamed about them falling, drowning, your hands reached out in panic and came up empty.

The airline was unpredictable. Twice it didn't show up at all and left you stranded at the airport. Later, on a rare week when it did come, you boarded the rickety plane—a fifty-minute flight to the neighboring town—the loneliness of staying outweighed your morbid fear of Zambian aircraft. You flew off looking down at the great distances, the ruts, the rivers that held you in, and Africa seemed small and insignificant, an optical illusion that lasted only as long as the flight.

For six months each year the great Zambezi Floodplain was dry and passable by four-wheel drive. Then you had a choice. Ten hours north to the Lukulu pontoon. You drove aboard a wooden ferry. Four men paddled you across the Zambezi River, a rope strung across the waters for a guide. The current was strong. The sun was hot. They navigated across and over to the opposite steep bank where you drove off into more sand.

Or you went the opposite direction and drove ten hours south to the Senanga pontoon. There you did the same ferry trick. North or south, you could take your pick. The opposite of everything was the same. There was sand no matter where you looked.

The Dutch government offered to repair a broken pontoon on the Zambezi River straight east. It would have cut the drive in half if it had been fixed.

It wasn't.

Dear Mom and Dad,

Johan found a farmer who brings me milk. I'm so glad to have it! Now I can make butter, yogurt, and cream cheese. Grandma would be proud of me!

I sieve out the hair and dirt before I boil it. The doctor told me twenty minutes will kill T.B.

Johan is very busy with his new job and he's gone a lot. He doesn't have a phone or anything. I never know when he'll be back home. He's been gone three days and two nights. It gives me lots of time to read.

Four workmen came today to paint our ceiling. They painted directly over the electrical cords, spiders, webs, and any bug that was in their path. There are little white bug lumps up there now. I watched for awhile; the bugs left slender trails behind as they crawled to and fro. After awhile they became disoriented and moved in circles while they slowly died.

I have to get going. I need to gather the chickens' eggs before dusk. If I leave them out too long they'll attract the cobras. YIKES!

Love you,
Jill

KALABO POST OFFICE WAS A DREARY SMALL BUILDING with paint fallen off in patchy chunks that left irregular bald holes in the crumbling cement. It was a mile or two from your house. To cheer yourself on the lonely walk you whistled. It sounded like your dad woodworking in his shop, whistling his only sound.

You stood in line, bought a stamp. Glue bushes lined the path outside. You picked a flower. White milkweed type sap dripped out, sticky and turning your fingers brown. You dripped it onto the corner of the envelope and affixed a stamp, hoping the glue would hold long enough for the letters to reach their destinations.

You walked back home empty-handed with your fingers smudged and sticky. As you walked you whistled once again. Chin-up, cheer-up, whistle while you walked. Maybe tomorrow a letter would come. Maybe tomorrow would be a better day.

People looked at you awry. You wondered why and asked. No one really said.

You asked again and after much coaxing and cajoling were told: people whistle when they're thinking dirty thoughts.

Poor you, you didn't know. You walked back and forth silently, weekly, for six years looking for connections between continents that seemed spaced farther away than Earth to Pluto.

And on that far-away planet things carried on while you were absent and departed—two words that are often used to refer to the dead. Your brother got married. He sent a picture of this bride you'd never met. Your sister had a baby and sent pictures of your mom and dad holding their new granddaughter. Your brother's wife had a baby. More pictures of the proud grandparents. You had a baby of your own. Then two. There are no pictures of your parents holding your newborns.

You sent padded envelopes full of pictures off to your folks: pictures of Johan in the fields, Johan teaching farmers, and Johan holding his newborn daughter. A year later he held a son. You wanted to capture happy moments to reassure your parents that you were fine and life was good. Maybe it was yourself you were trying to convince.

Your mom sent you a knit one-piece baby suit. It was exquisite.

She wrote, "Melinda will look so pretty in it."

Your floors were dirty cement with red floor polish. The suit was white.

Dear Mom and Dad,

It's been nearly four months now since I heard anything from you! The government still hasn't paid the airlines. So the plane service has been completely abandoned. There are rumors that the Zambian government is going bankrupt.

The Post Office finally sent a boat to Mongu to pick up the mail. It's a twelve-hour trip one way down river. It took three days for it to return. Empty. The Post Master in Mongu refused to send the mail. He said he wasn't allowed to put it on a boat because it was all stamped "Air Mail."

Good Grief!

Jill

THINGS THEY DID NOT HAVE IN KALABO VILLAGE: cards, flower shops, theaters, restaurants, movies. Bookstores, television, roller rinks. Carnivals, orchestras, symphonies. Higher education courses, community parks, city tournaments. Baseball, softball, stadiums, recreational facilities. Libraries. In short, what you were *used* to. You left all that behind the day you married.

You hardly had a honeymoon. All you did was work. In truth you hardly knew how to stand. But there was little place for mourning then, overwhelmed with survival. Who had time to contemplate? Feed the guests; nurse the babies; dysentery today, and hepatitis next. And now—after twenty-six years—you find yourself sorrowing over that time and place. Johan regrets part of the past and that helps. But still, hard as your try to forget, here it is again: a memory, a dream, a whisper in your mind. It comes back unaltered, unasked for in a clap of thunder or a handful of sand, a memory of a memory that will not be erased.

Go back, dig up what was buried there, and look at the face beneath the made-up grin, under the open-hearted philanthropic smile. Go back and see the tears brimming in your eyes. Watch them fall. Taste the salt. Underneath it all a question hides. Was God there? You felt so all alone.

And you wonder if Job was ever able to join his first and second lives. Did he think about his first twelve children who all died on the same day? And later when he had another batch of sons and daughters and when the third and then the fourth generations were born, did Job ever need to go back and mourn his suffering? Did he grieve the actual process that his losses set in motion?

Dear Mom and Dad,

It's a miracle. Or at least that is the way it feels after six long months!

We've got mail! The doctor went in person all the way to Mongu to get it.

I have half a dozen packages from you on my table. Thank you so much! I'm so happy to have them even though they got absolutely soaked in diesel. It smells like a gas station in my house! But I only had to throw away the Jell-O boxes. The rest was salvageable. And most of the letters are readable. The spaghetti has bugs in it, but I can sieve them out after I boil the noodles. If all else fails I'll just pick them out. This is a skill I've newly become quite deft at.

Our mattresses got infested with bedbugs or lice or something. I hauled them all out in the sun and washed all the laundry. Johan says he thinks the lice came from the chickens.

Then last week during the night the Itezi ants came through. Millions of them marching in a straight line. When I woke up it was quiet. No chickens squawking. I went out to the coop and it was disgusting. All my chickens and ducks were gone, honestly only a heap of bones remaining. Poor things were eaten alive. I hadn't heard any commotion in the night. Did they die silently? I looked around and could see the straggling end of the army ant lines. They had marched straight through our house.

Johan says, "Look at the bright side. They ate all the cockroaches. Besides no more lice, right?"

Love,

Jill

FOR YEARS AFTER I CAME BACK I made lists: numerous, long lists that were my vain attempt to find resolution and lay the past aside. *Count Your Blessings Name Them One by One* was the first list. I could have just as easily counted my bitterness. The two were woven well together. The second list I tried was *Things God Taught Me When*. But I grew tired of this inventory of teachable moments and soon began another: *Perseverance Builds Character*.

My lists were good for sorting, classifying, and containing. This was really what I wanted to do. I wanted to control Africa. I wanted to put those years in a box and close the lid. I peppered my lists with fragmented Bible verses of the *My-ways-are-not-your-ways* sort. But like Lazareth—called out of the tomb before the grave cloth was ripped off his eyes—I was still in the dark.

I dug out those old blue aerogrammes and read between the lines. I searched through hidden wounds—a pen my probe—and wrote the story I hadn't told. The honest middle part: Job in chapter two . . . and three . . . and four. I wrote fractured essays and threw them out at the world. The essays were filled with wandering thoughts and the paths that life had placed me on. The writing of this splintered unknowing became my respite.

I began another list. I called it *Just Because I Don't Know Doesn't Mean I'm Stupid*. It filled up quickly. There was so much in Africa I couldn't comprehend. Where did that wonderful plan go? I filled in the list—page after page full of what I didn't understand: refugees, kwashiorkor, starvation. Flash flood kills British friend's two toddlers. Robberies, deceptions, despotism. Dutch neighbor's baby born and lives one hour in Kalabo Hospital, blue while father and friend desperately try to resuscitate. Drought, bribery, tribalism.

The bare mention of these facts dislodges my heart. If I go back too far I sink into the sand of the Kalahari: there is no way out.

Canadian dad watches crocodile kill sixteen-year-old son then walks barefoot through the night through the bush to get home to tell the mother. Blindness, insanity, corruption. Elderly village man struck by truck in front of house loses both legs in a bloody pulpy heap. Leprosy, orphans, polio, measles, AIDS. The storms on Sunshine Mountain hide my view.

Maybe I climbed the wrong mountain. Maybe not.

There is turbulence on every peak, and turmoil, and tumult. Bluster, broil, and brawl. All hell let loose. God shelters in the storm, obscured.

I am caught in this contradictory fraction of a second, wedged in a moment of waiting. Like Lazareth I am simultaneously called forth and blind. He holds his hands out in front of his cloth-wrapped face and feels his way towards the voice.

A snarled grave cloth is wrapped around my head, covering my eyes, blinding me. I stand with my hands outstretched and holding stories. I touch the doorway of the tomb. The stone is rolled away. I search towards the opening.

PATER NOSTER DON THOMPSON

Our Father who
    and how
      could anyone sane imagine omniscience
                    in trousers
        worn out shiny khaki perhaps
        with feet in white work socks
              up on a coffee table
    littered with how-to mags such as
                Popular Creation
and come to Him boldly saying
      "Abba,
      Father,
      everything is possible for You"

Once long ago a wife and I babysat a boy whose mother had died recently, whose father was trying to finish grad school anyway and then return home to Turkey; and the boy who had not one word in common with us huddled all day in a corner crying out, "Baba! Baba!" We could do nothing for him,

        Father
    and therefore if You

art in heaven
    how can we wanting so much to be
            close to You
        tolerate where we are now
      here in this
            abattoir
            with no Abba

        in which we look for You
                it seems in vain
    or so say best-selling Dawkins Harris Hitchens
                so sane
    and all defunct nontheists from
                Diagoras to sad Madeleine
    though Nietzsche at least
                understood
            what it would mean
    muttering disconsolation through a soup strainer
            if God were
                not in heaven
            but dead

Last summer when Bogdan whacked Jerzy with a vodka bottle, he bled all over our front porch before the cops came and the EMTs and the ambulance that took him away; nothing serious: a few stitches; but one of the cops leaving advised me to hose off the concrete quickly: "Nothing can wash away blood stains"

                of bomb splatter
              or wife knifings
                      of endless carnage
          geopolitical
          or personal
                Your blood too
Lamb led to the slaughter

hallowed be Thy name
        who died bloody
                inconceivably lacerated

When those red zone Presa Canarios, crazier haters than any Roman soldiers with their short swords and short pay stuck in a verminous, god-infested backwater—when those two mad dogs in San Francisco finished with Miss Whipple, nothing remained unmutilated, the coroner said, except the soles of her feet

PATER NOSTER

                shredded
           for our sins
         yes
but also risen for us and for our redemption
           Abba
            Father
              for whom everything is
        possible but
how can anyone sane imagine omniscience
                  slaughtered
            like Miss Whipple or
      vaporized like Iraqis
out buying their daily bread
                unless
              for You
        death is no hindrance
no more than air is for the birds
            the element in which
          You rise
so that we see You scintillant above us
not going south
        as anyone sane would
                like a goose out of Gethsemane
                      and well rid of
        this hideousness
but coming
again for us so that

Thy kingdom come, Thy will be done
                whether or not
              we know it
          when we see it or
              can do the math
one and one and one adding up to one
        to balance the books with
                in the debit column
the body count

       insane
       obscene
"in the midst of life we are in death"
     and who can guess how many souls
       pack hell
        like beans in
          an infinite jar
or how many rungs the angels must climb
    on Jacob's ladder
who has looked over Your shoulder
        Father
    while You crunched the numbers
wearing a green eyeshade
     not plastic
      but translucent emerald
using an ancient calculator
     with a lever
       like a slot machine
each pull subtotaling a century
on earth as it is in heaven

Give us this day our daily bread
        without grit in it
          please
     for once without
   blood in the dough
without apocalyptic warnings on the label
     overpopulation
     global warming
     bird flu
   no mystery for once
just plain bread and

forgive us our trespasses as we
    litigious down to our hammer toes
  throw stones first and last

PATER NOSTER

        tuning in to
    cable channel *Schadenfreude*

Here's Britney on the gurney with her blemished skin and eyes like an injured dog who shouldn't have survived that idiotic attempt to chase debauchery across a busy street; and here come the commentators—shrinks, moralists, do-gooders, freaks who got over it, all eager to tell us too much about what we don't need to know

    who have our own unremarkable debauches
        refusing to
forgive those who trespass against us

And lead us not into
        endless dead ends
        sloughs of despond
        wildernesses of
temptation

but deliver us from
    faux sane self-obsessed poisonous piety
        from our wiles
        and woes
            from
    in other words
  ourselves

the evil one.

Amen.

MIDRIFT LYN HAWKS

Sometimes lately when I stand up too sudden, my vision gets dark around the edges, like a tunnel's creeping in from all sides. It's how they say it is when you have the near-death experience and then rush back from heaven with the light warming your back. At first I hated being dizzy but now I don't want to come out of it, same as when your eyes glaze over at the computer, how you see but not see. Psychologists say go find that restful place in your head, so I got my own strange versions of the ocean scene to run to. I got me the dizzy place, and I got me a touched-up photo from Memory Lane. That's where I picture me landing behind Daddy's little shotgun house in Jackson, fixed up nice, where the paint don't peel and the color is turquoise, bright as those scarab beetles in Monique's books about Egypt. The grass shimmers like angels just dusted it and there's a red, red rose bush dead center where there used to be scabby lawn full of bald patches. I tell myself, that rose bush is Mama, just blooming away, right out of Daddy's ash heap.

Lord, I can't afford dizzy today. You got to be on when you take on the Academy. You're staring down brick and stone and columns and miles of flowers, so much I never stop expecting guards with hats like Buckingham.

I pull in the circle drive and just about run into the stone lion when I see what they got on patrol today: Little Miz Tramp, strutting up the front walk like a ho. Skirt's seven inches above the knee and shirt's two inches above the navel. Somebody get me a ruler. Does this school want Britney Spears sashaying around here? Where is the supervision, I ask you.

She cuts her eyes over here at the Caprice Classic clunking over speed bumps. This thing wants me in real deep debt. I'm going to park this fender-bender right between this silver Audi and that gold Lexus SUV. Every car here got vanity plates in code, like BLKD . . . something, whatever the hell that means.

I hoof it to the front door, my midsection wobbling like sweaty Jell-O. Least I don't have to sweat my way past Britney; she and her stomach staples went MIA. Damn, already 12:07: this lunch break they give you is hardly enough time to order up heartburn. My ribs grip me like a cage; any breath that's left is locked up tight.

Inside, everywhere you look is beige, beige, *beige* linoleum and white walls, whiter than Whole Foods on a Saturday. Tell me why the kids get stuck in these Novocain barracks while the admin crib gets the Taj Mahal columns and hardwood floors? You wouldn't think this place cost 13G a year. I never can remember where the damn office is. Everything's underground and understood. Now I'm feeling my acid reflux start to simmer.

A bathroom says "Faculty Women" so I scoot inside, overheated with flashbacks, like what Uncle Franklin used to joke was his Post-Dramatic Mess. I splash water on my face and blink a few times to clear the fog of memories crawling up on me. End of my eighth grade year, I swore to Mama I'd just as soon firebomb Suffolk High as go there. I begged to go live with Daddy. All she said was, "His house been repossessed." No word on him, mind you, just, *you got no place to go*. Till then it called to me like Fantasy Island, like a box of teal ocean ready to cool my brow. At thirteen I was too stupid, thinking I could make threats and Mama would just forget. So I won me an all-expense-paid vacation straight to Uncle Franklin's where I just about sweat out ten pounds picking tobacco in Tarboro. Dripping at sunrise, dripping at supper, grabbing and snapping and tucking leaves all day. Black gum under your nails and in the cracks of your hands. Then I got nicotine poisoning shoving the leaves up under my arm. I never said another word about Suffolk after that, even though food ran through me like water every damn morning till graduation. Too bad it don't do that now.

I blot my face, put on some lipstick, and suck a shot from my inhaler. That would be my yoga breath for the day. I tell the mirror, "You are looking at the admin assistant to the CFO of WireTech." That would be my mantra. I check my arms; no soak-through yet on this new silk blouse, praise Jesus, two-for-one sale at T. J. Maxx. Put on your shield, Mama used to say every day; I couldn't look at her, I'd be so mad, but wouldn't you know, she's still right.

I tell her, "My baby's mixed up in some kind of disciplinary incident. This is a first, Mama; you know that."

I come out the bathroom and right by me goes Li'l Miz Ho. Oooh, yes, honey!—caught by some teacher, asking her why she's violating dress code. This school's finally cracking down on the rising tide of midriff tees. Ms. Thang starts her whining but Teacher's ready for her—tall skinny woman with a butch haircut—saying go change right now or we call your mom. Either way she gets detention. Britney huffs away to get the alleged sweatshirt. Teacher watches her go, making sure she makes it there. Rules is rules, little girl.

If there's one thing you won't catch Monique doing, it's this midriff shit. I haven't smacked her in years but she knows I'll take up the habit if I see her baring and sharing. One time she tried to leave the house in one of those lacy-racy, spaghetti-strap tees, looking like a bony bird poking out that piece of lingerie. We had us a little meeting. Now she covers up with a cardigan, still tight as they come, but she keeps that thing ON. I tell her, "Should I get a call from this school saying someone saw your navel, you know I don't play."

A bell goes "ting," some New-Age sound, and the halls fill up with chatter, and then the swarm comes. An ocean of Abercrombie and Fitch, Lord have mercy. I swim upstream to get at this teacher and holler at her I'm looking for Donna Kennedy.

The woman flashes me a big, horsy smile. "I'm Donna Kennedy. You must be Antoinette Mabry." Now it'd be real funny if I was like, "Naw, I'm Britney's mama." There's only one bite of chocolate running around this sophomore class.

"Mama!" Someone grabs me from behind, got me in a vice grip. I turn around and hold her tight. If Monique's not afraid to hug me in front of God and everyone, then I *know* something's wrong.

"What is going on?" Monique shakes her head and swipes at her face. Ms. Kennedy points us to a little hallway.

"Go on, Mama, I'll sit here." Monique plops on a chair, faced away from the crowd, her bright eyes crusty.

"You sure?"

She swallows hard. I better go before she busts out crying in front of these people.

Ms. Kennedy's wall says she's a counselor with degrees from somewhere up north, she played college ball, and she birthed two Ross Perot babies, so ugly they're cute. She has me sit on a love seat near a box of Kleenex. She's standing like she's forgetting something.

"Excuse me just one second," she says, laughing through her words the way nervous white people do.

"There's been a cruel prank," she says when she comes back. She shuts the door and plunks herself in her chair. She's got a man's body, clamping her legs like she don't know how to cross them. "Ten girls in the sophomore class received hate letters in their lockers. We believe they were placed early this morning."

I shake my head, suck my teeth. My heart's pounding a drum solo. "I told y'all to let these kids have locks." It's this stupid kumbaya community shit they got going, people all up in each other's personal property. Monique's "lost," what, at least five books now? That damn chemistry book cost near sixty dollars and the scholarship don't pay for that. Tell me why in God's name do *these* kids need to steal. And now we've got a hate crime? I'm telling you what.

"What's the content of these letters?" Do not use contractions, I tell myself.

"They're very troubling." Ms. Kennedy catches herself looking at her desk. There's a pile of papers with some funky-ass print. These kids got computer access 24/7, so when they blackmail each other they can do it up nice in Macaroni font.

"Basically, the letters threaten each girl, and they reveal personal information, and—"

"Threaten how?" Damn, Antoinette, don't interrupt!

"With . . . rape, basically."

Say what? "I beg your pardon?"

"Yes, it's very upsetting. We're bringing in a detective. The language *sounds* 'male,'" she holds up long fingers to make quote marks, "but we're not sure it isn't a girl."

My mind's spinning. Number one, ten girls are mixed up in this. That means they can't just put it on Monique.

Number two, it may not be a boy. She sure as hell don't need some Ted Bundy stalking her—give me a psycho slut any day. It's probably Britney Spears, and Monique can take her. Before I went to Suffolk, girls at the public junior high would just as soon pull out your hair than pass you a hate note. Least Monique don't have to deal with that.

"We've been searching all the lockers," Ms. Kennedy's saying. "But that was after Monique discovered a letter in her locker—on her own, around 8:45. She came right to us. So we think the incident occurred some time between 8:00 and 8:30, when everyone was in class . . ."

Monique, what the hell you think you were doing in that hallway out of class? She better feel the darts shooting at her from this office. My daughter's too smart to pull this shit, but this school never gets the news flash. Just waiting for her to mess up.

"I need to see this letter," I say.

Surprise, surprise, she hands it over. It's typical white girl shit, how you're fat and ugly and "I'm going to rape you ten million times till you die." Then something about how Bryant and Leon are saying they've already "done you twice." Bryant, he's that one always harassing the other black male, Leon, telling him he too white, he a prep, when Bryant's black ass been playing tennis his whole damn life up at the club. Just because Bryant listens to that Ludacris shit don't make him ghetto. What's got my baby in tears is people saying she lost it to them two. Maybe I ought to tell her how—no. Kid doesn't need Mama whining about sticks and stones of yesteryear.

"The girls' friendships are a bit broken up right now, but we're going to restore our community." I just give Kennedy a look. That's not all that's broke; Monique's been shivering on her skinny-ass piece of ice with the sharks circling since she started here. How is today any different? Kennedy's saying she'll be counseling all of them starting tomorrow. My baby's hurting *now*. I stand up.

"I need to see about my daughter. Please call me if you learn anything new."

"Of course. We're advocating strict consequences, Mrs. Mabry—"

"Ms.," I say. "They don't believe in punishment around here."

She looks all butch and helpless. She knows I speak the truth. That thing last year on the senior class trip where they trashed a hotel in Virginia Beach: all those kids got was a slap on the wrist. Mama and me now, we would have set up a Woodshed Holiday Inn to host their asses, belts and brushes and switches. They'd never sit down again.

I ask, to help her out, "Did you send her to lunch?"

"Yes, I did. And—yes."

"Will she pass back this way?"

"Yes." She looks like she swallowed something nasty and is trying to cover it up.

I say goodbye. I've got fifteen minutes. Should have had Monique get me something from that cafeteria because otherwise all I got time for is some Nabs, not exactly the Atkins special. I cross the main hall and sit down outside the office to wait.

You try to do the right thing. You really do. Monique don't know a lot about how I worry. Like this one coming along here, this kind she goes to school with, what I call Shaggy. I see him stumbling in if I drop her off late. Can't open his eyes, all grunge with his shirt flapping and laces flopping. Squeals into the parking lot, the Jeep with huge antenna, coked up some days, stoned others. No one cares about his ass, the parents always in Europe, Monique says. He lurches into the office and signs in; it's been a liquid lunch if you ask me. A twenty flutters out his sagging britches. A freshman pacing around this hallway dragging his roller backpack, the Urkel Special, he lunges to pick it up. Shaggy waves him off. That's how you know when a kid is using. He walks in here with more Gs than my monthly salary. It's one fine ride downhill.

So you got the drug runners and then you got the bulimic debs, those girls Monique hangs with. They're like Saran Wrap, nothing to them. They're like a cult: once you're in, till death do us part. Monique says she can hang with anyone, she's friends with all the groups, but what if she's caught up in some Meow Mix I don't know about? These girls, they make a list, and then they cross people *out*.

Lord, girl, Mama says over my shoulder, *don't kill yourself. That child's going to be fine. Look what you went through. You turned out all right.*

Monique also don't know how I check that grades website two, three times a day, like it's the Dow Jones. Hell, she *is* my investment. *You worth more than a mortgage!* I always tell her when she say, *Mama, why don't we just get us a house?* Says she'll go on back to Carthage. Not when she's doing so good, never below a B. Mama was so proud last fall when Monique made it in, after wait list hell freshman year, dodging all that trash back at public. Mama, if I'd known how bad off you was, I would have sounded more positive. At the time I said, *Get back to me in June.* But she had to part with us before Thanksgiving, only one of Monique's grade reports in hand. We buried it with her. Monique don't know that.

"Antoinette!" says a voice acting BBC. Thelma Covington, Bryant's mama. Lord, take me now.

"Girl, how you *doing?*" She stands over me, hair the latest Halle Berry, suit one of those Vogue tweedy fringe specials looking like it needs hemming.

"Just fine, fine." Look at me squealing back. "How you?"

"Just *perfect!* Listen, did Monique tell you we're having a movie night Saturday?"

"No, she did not. Isn't that nice."

"Well, we sure hope she can come! She's just a gorgeous girl. Stunning!" The woman's got a voice could kill dogs. While she's gushing, she's halfway inside the office chatting up the secretary and sniffing out awards for her son.

Make me sick. She and all her other PTA carbon copies acting like they're soul food, slave-history black. That gold Lexus and the code license plate come together—it said, BLKDVA. Is she for real? Let me retch right here.

As I was saying: you got the stoners, the debs, and now the cherry on top, the faux noirs. A nest of vipers is what it is. Go on now, call me a hypocrite: I'm always dropping Monique off at some function Thelma's kid throws in Better-Than-You North Raleigh. But how can I say no to my baby making friends, as long as she's not getting drunk or worse over there. Which she does not. You got to ask yourself, what's worse: this, or what I went through. First day of my freshman year at Suffolk, I see some cracker-ass senior wearing the Confederate flag like a cape. And then that Jewish guy, Horowitz, one lunchtime just like this: I'm walking with the only Korean and Mexican on the whole damn campus, he's walking with some new-money rednecks in their Carolina ball caps and Skynyrd shirts. He says like a megaphone, "Here comes the dog parade!" I turn and holler, "There go the asshole!" Then the Suffolk sayonara, *Ripley's Believe it or Not*, is I had to shake *Jesse Helms'* damn hand at graduation. That racist motherfucker helped our boys into West Point while he was doing his filibuster on the Dr. King Holiday. Shameful. When he beat Gantt's ass in '90, Mama cried.

Transpose '86 and you get the year I was born. Tell me, how were things different then than the year King got shot? Mama would swear light years of difference, but I beg to differ. That would be the sum total of my nostalgia for Suffolk Class of '86.

Kids come through the double doors from lunch, more with roller backpacks, half their asses out of dress code. Here's my baby, carrying nothing but ice cream, one of those Nutty Buddy things. She's swiping at her face, fresh wet, and I see some dandruff we didn't get, little snow flecks in her chignon she wears all the time now.

"That it for lunch?"

"I'm not hungry. You want it, Mama?"

I take it. She sinks into the seat next to me. I find her a Kleenex. She pulls out her make-up and gets herself fixed.

"I guess they're going to ask me some questions," she says.

"Why?"

"I don't know, they're going to talk to each one of us."

Her shoulders look like two little knobs hunched up. She used to have more meat on her.

"You the first to go in?"

"Yeah."

"When?"

"In a few minutes."

The first to find the thing. The first to get questioned. The usual suspect . . . my stomach does a backflip. "Where's your principal—what's his name again?"

"Mr. Millipan. Mama, what you going to do?"

I stride into the big office. The secretary's a pudge-face woman with kinky gray hair that won't bob the way she wants; no lips, they're pressed in so tight. This one hates her job but hates people more.

"I need to see Mr. Millipan," I tell her.

"Do you have an appointment?" Won't even look at me, all about her computer screen.

"No, but this concerns an emergency."

She click-click-clicks on her little screen in super slo-mo.

"He can see you at three-thirty tomorrow."

She's got my sign—A LACK OF PREPARATION ON YOUR PART DOES NOT CONSTITUTE AN EMERGENCY ON MINE—behind her desk. Least mine's framed and not tacked up on some lame-ass corkboard.

"He can see me now," I tell her, "before he interrogates my daughter."

Light in those beady blue eyes. *Oh, the parent of the criminal.* Just the way she likes black people.

"Well, I'm very sorry, he'll be available at three-thirty *tomorrow*."

I turn to a door without a nameplate. "Is this his office?"

She glares. I knock.

"Excuse me!" Beady Eyes yelps.

"Mama!" Monique hollers.

"Come in," says a faint voice. I open the door.

I've seen this man before. He always looks tall and too skinny, like his pants about to slip off. A good head of gray hair but no chin. Always smiling. He's squinting at his computer, and when he swivels in his chair, he smiles big though he don't know me.

"May I help you?"

"Mr. Millipan," Beady Eyes whines, "I tried to tell her—"

He jumps up, rubbing his hands. "Ah, well, Mrs. Cerban, I'm sure we can work this out."

Mrs. Cerban's a little purple around the edges. She stomps away.

"I'm Antoinette Mabry, mother of Monique Mabry," I tell him. He shuts us in. I shove the ice cream in my purse. "My daughter received one of these letters. What is this investigation?"

"Yes, of course. Rich Millipan." He extends a long, ladyfinger hand. I shake it. Moist. "Please sit down." Another love seat waiting on me; this place's just full of love.

"I understand my daughter's about to be questioned." This office makes me claustrophobic, crammed full of art and books.

"Yes, we're going to speak with each of the girls." He puts his fingers together like a church steeple.

My heart's about to bust out of my chest. "Will she be alone?"

Mr. Millipan leans forward, smiling like he's surprised. I smell me some nerves. "Usually it would be myself and the dean of students there."

"Would be or will be?"

He blinks. "Will be."

"Will she have an advocate?" Now that's a gem I pulled out of nowhere.

"You mean, such as her academic advisor?"

Whoever that is. Monique don't talk about that. I know she likes some teachers and some she don't. "Yes, or a teacher she trusts. Or myself."

"We usually provide an advocate should a student face the Honor Council. But since this is a preliminary investigation, we just need to ask her a few questions."

Come on down to the station, boy. We just need to ask you a few questions. The soundtrack of the streets of South Raleigh. My sweat's damn near destroying this blouse.

"I understand that a girl may be the perpetrator," I say. His eyes widen; I bet Butch Kennedy wasn't supposed to let that out. "I don't want Monique to be alone when she's questioned. I need your guarantee she won't be accused, being that she was the first to discover a letter and what have you." Lord, am I making sense?

"This is simply informational questioning, Mrs. Mabry."

"Ms., if you please. There's always going to be a bias, Mr. Millipan. Will she have an advocate?"

"I understand your concern—"

"I got a few others, too." Damn, chill. I can feel Mama hovering, ready to smack me. "I need to know why Monique has to be the first."

"We like to get right on these things before the students get too stirred up. We—"

"Things is already stirred." Now he's got owl eyes. Righteous anger runs my engine now.

"I understand you all went through the student lockers already." I can hear Mama behind me. *Go on, girl, say it.*

"Well, Mrs. Mabry," he harrumphs, because he don't handle pit bulls too well, "I don't like to speculate about student rumors."

"But you just said you're rushing things to avoid the rumors spreading."

We're eying each other, and he looks real stupid, deer with no chin caught in headlights. I think he forgot the question. So I say it again.

"I need to know if Monique will have an advocate."

"Well, that really hasn't ever been our procedure—"

"I think it's time it was."

"Mrs. Mabry, our policy is a result of committee study and faculty approval. I cannot reverse our policies on my own. We have a democratic process at Cheshire."

Now that's too funny, but I don't laugh. Democratic for everybody save the damn kids.

"What if the policy puts the students in—" I'm hurting for words here. "—an unsafe position?" Is *unsafe* in the dictionary?

"Monique will be safe. We value her."

My ass you do. In these kinds of investigations, detectives are always looking for the one on the fringe. It sure as hell ain't my baby, wasn't ever me, but who the hell you think they questioned first when a rich white girl named Pinky helped herself to everyone's shit back at Suffolk? Mmm-hmm. *My* black ass.

I take a deep breath. "If you value her, give her an advocate."

A small vein's throbbing in his temple. "I understand your position, but there is nothing I can do to change things at this time."

"You're the principal."

The vein jumps like a gymnast. "Mrs. Mabry, I do not appreciate your tone."

"And I don't appreciate this investigation. You can interview her like I just said or I'm taking her home."

Do I mean home for the day? Home for good? Because I don't know where we go from here.

Little beads of sweat like a pearl mustache on his upper lip as he says, "I don't think things need to go this way." I'm not sure why I make him so nervous; it's not like I hold a wad of Gs over his head like some. Maybe the federal government's got them hog-tied; they can't get some kind of funds unless they have enough scholarship chocolate spread around here.

"Well, that's where they're going because I will not have her rights violated like this." I stand up to place a period right where he can see it.

"Mrs. Mabry, let's not leave things this way. Please sit down." He tries to wipe himself off without me seeing, but it's pitiful, it truly is. And then I understand. This is not just a weak man: this is a man with some *guilt*. It's the Martin Luther King, Jr. poster on his wall next to the *All Are Welcome Here* rainbow poster for the fags. The gold-letter, hardback copy of *To Kill a Mockingbird* center stage on his bookshelf. That book and *Huck Finn* were the only "sympathy" we got in English class back in the day. The rest was string-'em-up-high *Heart of Darkness* shit. Then low on his totem pole is the Harvard diploma, way below eye level, like he's ashamed. He's got a bad case of bleeding heart, we've-done-the-Negro-wrong kind of guilt. He's just the right generation, too, maybe ten- or twenty-some years older than me. One of those who sits at home watching the riots every few years, wringing his hands.

We have ourselves a moment of silence while he's stressing.

I help him along. "Do you know why the faculty won't give the students an advocate?"

"I couldn't tell you." Look at him, he's just wiped out. This man could never handle the drugs and guns they got at Carthage; and they call this man the *principal*. But he looks relieved he's fessed up.

"Let me ask you this," I say. "Can it *hurt?*"

"Frankly, I don't see how it can. It's just a matter of . . . coordination—"

"A small thing," I interrupt, my voice soft, "when you think about it." I'm trying to stroke the idea, because really, this right here is something for the record books, something for Mama to see. A white man in his fifties intimidated by *me*. If only she had the pleasure.

"Perhaps this time you can have a private-type, you know, arrangement, a kind of exception or what have you . . . maybe a trial run. Maybe just see how it goes."

His eyes are right with me, a new light shining. I just gave him a hole he can crawl out. He's babbling, "Well, Mrs. Mabry, that's a fine idea. We might just try that."

That's right, it's time you started making some exceptions. But I can feel Mama shaking her head behind me, breath pushed out like wind. Mama, come on, now! I've got to get us something here for all you never had. What else you want?

"I'm sure Monique's advisor or maybe a particular teacher would be willing to help out . . ." Leaving me out as an option. But that's all right, that's all right, we've made some progress here.

"That sounds like a wonderful plan," I tell him. It's done. Someone's a witness to my baby's interrogation. No one can sub in for Antoinette Mabry, but this individual will be hearing from me before and after, as close as I can get to the trial, even if I have to rehearse with this advocate person. I bite my tongue to keep from saying thank you. Mama always did, but I make a point not to thank when the things should be a guarantee.

I say, "May I see the list of questions?"

"I'm afraid not. I hope you understand we need to keep things confidential."

Fine, fine. Let him feel like he won something. Like these girls don't talk! But Monique won't be confiding in nobody.

There it goes, that stupid bell.

"Well, Mr. Millipan, if she has an advocate, I'm comfortable with you asking her some questions with that advocate there. May she go find her advocate now?" I like saying the word, it's like sucking on that dark Ghirardelli chocolate. An aftertaste of bittersweet, though. I wonder what's getting to me: maybe I barked so loud I scared myself.

"Yes, well, fine, perhaps that's the best idea," he's saying. And just like that, we pull her out of first place. Let someone else blaze the damn trail while Monique gets herself some backup. I nominate Britney.

I can see his mind starting to turn all of a sudden, hit upside the head with, *What did I just do? What if the other girls hear?* Mister, that's your problem now.

I stand up, smooth my skirt, hold out my hand. He leaps up. We shake. "I'm going to get Monique on to class. Please call me tonight to let me know the latest." Meanwhile, I am so late for work Monique won't be seeing me till after seven.

"Will do, Mrs. Mabry. We'll do our best to take care of things. I'm so glad we had this chat."

"Thank you," I say. Damn, that one sneaked out, but I am thankful, Jehovah Jira thankful, that my baby's left alone. "Goodbye." And it really is, because you will never see me here again.

I stride by Beady Eyes and out the door. I tell Monique to follow me.

Outside school we sit on a bench. Cold air feels good and fresh out here, don't petrify my lungs. I hug her, then keep my hand between her shoulders, firm. We need to pump up these muscles and get her back in competition shape. But first I'm going to get some answers.

"It wasn't me, Mama."

"Why in Jesus name would I think it was you?"

"I know, but—"

"Don't you *ever* think I don't trust you." I grab her chin, look her in the eye, then kiss her face hard. "You know what I don't trust. All you got to tell me is why you were in that damn hallway this morning."

"Getting my binder! I couldn't find my English homework, so I had to pull everything out of my locker."

I believe her.

She hunches over again. "I hate this place."

"You didn't yesterday." Yesterday it was nothing but rah-rah this and rah-rah that with cheerleading.

"OK, I hate Jennifer Beech."

"Mmm, let me guess. She the one in the midriff tee today. Three-inch heels?"

"Yeah."

"Thought so. Well, baby, what you going to do?" I want to say, *Why the hell you hang with Paris Hilton?* But her three years of teenager already schooled me you get more with honey.

"Lay low," she tells me. "Don't say nuthin'."

That's my baby. We're grinning at each other, because that's our little chant ever since we saw that video by The Roots, conscience rap, which if you ask me is what we need more of nowadays.

"Any idea why she do this?"

"She hate all the rest of us. She pretend she like us, but I was talking to Sara," now her voice shifts to café au lait, but she don't even hear it, "and it's like Jennifer's always spreading rumors about everyone else, and like what, do she think we don't know?" Now she's back, my bilingual baby. "She think she the queen, but . . ." Monique's cutting her eyes and blowing out her breath all disgusted.

"I know, these people beyond words sometimes. They call it 'leveling,'" I tell her. "Dr. Phil talked all about it other day on *Oprah*. Someone jealous of you, they got two choices: bring themselves up, or bring you down. But Martin Luther King said it best: 'the drum major instinct.'"

"Everyone else thinks it's Lanny or Smithy who did it."

"Smithy? What kind of name *that*?"

"*Mama*."

"I know, just playing." Hell, I went to school with boys named Winston the Third and Beverly James, a.k.a. BJ, I'm not lying, so no one needs to lecture me on freaky ass names for Southern men. "But you sure it's not the boys now."

"Did you see the letters?"

"Yeah, I know that's right. I saw the one you got."

She looks embarrassed, so I look away. That thing about Bryant and Leon, damn those fools. I bet they're always talking shit about her fine ass anyway, so you know it's all hit a little too close to home.

"Or," Monique's saying, this thoughtful look on her face, "it's Emily."

Emily's that little mousy thing who is as fringe as fringe can get. Her parents are some kind of sprout-eating hippies stuck in 1972. She's mixed, the sad kind, with that wide yellow nose, nappy, worthless hair, and a bad case of acne.

"Yeah, she wishes she was Jennifer. She's like *obsessed*." And Monique's sigh is deep, twenty thousand leagues deep, like she can see from here to Mama's eternity. And I see all of a sudden that Jennifer's the easy target for us to shoot. That diva's way too busy with her own self to mess with anyone else. It's the fringe kid who feels it raw like a blade to the gut, to where she hates everyone as much as I did. Yes, the outsider can think up some sick shit in their spare time.

My baby, she's so smart. It'll take the detective ten days when it takes her less than ten minutes. But Monique don't look too pleased with herself. I can see she's worrying on Emily; she's what they call an empath, feeling what the others feel all the time. It's a gift but it's a curse. Damn, damn the weight of this anorexic, strung-out school. If she can just keep on keepin' on, Mama.

The cold gets to us a little, so I put my arm around her.

"What class you supposed to be in right now?"

"Ms. Droite."

"She the one that teach you how you oppressed?"

"No, Mama! She's my *history* teacher." Monique's got some theory-crazy English teacher who can wrap her lips around the word "oppression." What was it that woman told her, something about "three systems of oppression—class, race, and gender—that black women face vis-à-vis *A Raisin in the Sun*." Didn't *nobody* bring up that shit when I was in school.

"Mama," my own Beneatha's going on, "we have no idea what oppression really is. Oh my God, do you know what went on in *Mississippi* back in the day?" Apparently they're spending the required 2.5 days on the Movement now.

"You think North Carolina didn't have its mess *back in the day?*" The nerve of my child thinking some white woman's going to teach her where black folk supposed to be the most oppressed! I want to laugh. I read. I got my college prep on once, and I read all those books no one ever checked out at Suffolk. *Coming of Age in Mississippi* is back at the house, only Monique don't know that. I know all about some Freedom Summer and SNCC; where's she think Granddaddy's from? Where's she think SNCC got started? Shaw University, right on down the road, my alma mater when I finish. It's my turn to give my baby some homework. I may need to start with some stories about Suffolk. How it's more than just her rival and a far cry from any Freedom School. *My alma monster. Suffuck.* Time to share *all* those pet names.

"Girl," I say finally, because she's got to go to class and I've got to beg my job back, "I don't have much wisdom except a high school diploma. I don't have the college degree to swear to you it's all worth it, but you're going to do better than me. Of course now, I had you, best thing I ever did, and you know your daddy's proud of you, too." Damn straight he better be proud, though he never calls. Long as the child support keeps on keepin' on. "And you know how proud I am. Now if it gets too hateful here, then we pull you out, we save us some money, and we buy that home sooner rather than later. But if you think you can hang in, well . . ." Part of me feels guilt because I wish she'd say, "Get me out of here." *Come on, girl, do what I never got to do. Turn your back on these people for good. And then we can buy what we have my eye on; the little white house on the cul-de-sac that's two story and a big backyard and a door blue as Caribbean sky.*

Monique's eyes have dried up now and they've got the old look back. "White girls got the letter, too, Mama. It's an equal opportunity institution." She giggles.

"That's all there is here," I grump at her, "white chicks showing skin."

"Yeah, but you know what I mean."

"I know. You in The Club." I look at her, hard. "Don't you lose yourself now, you hear me?"

"*Mama, I hear you.*" Then she looks solemn, like she's already graduated the school of life. "It's like one of those foreign exchange programs." Now she gets her voice going half Valley Girl, half Tarboro twang. "Like, don't I, like, speak their language right pretty?" She's a mess.

"But I'm *fine*, Mama." Now she looks anxious because I'm not laughing. She wants to please me so bad it hurts. Now I got to make her laugh.

"Britney, she gon' get preg," I say. I'm hoping she'll pick up the joke we have about the fools on Court TV, always showing their dirty laundry—*Just like the world want to see niggers,* Mama used to say.

"She already been preg—and drunk," Monique says, giggling.

"I got preg," I say, punching her shoulder, "and a good thing that was, too."

"But you wadn't drunk," Monique says, and she's grinning more.

"Naw, naw," I say, but I can't look at her. Truth is I always was, back at Shaw, which is why my business never got finished. Monique, she don't get that choice. "Now I just scored you an advocate, so drag Ms. Trot's liberator ass into that meeting, you hear me? You say she's got your back?"

"*Mama!* It's Ms. Dro-o-ttt." She purrs out these French r's, looking frustrated. "She's cool, Mama."

"All right then. And remember, when someone asks you why you got yourself an advocate—"

"Don't say nuthin'." I hear a parrot, not my baby girl. She won't look at me now. Maybe she's guessed the rules of this game, the slippery slope up. Well, precious girl, it's an ugly sight when you look too close, but we're making it.

"All right, then." I've got to go. I dig for my keys, come up with the Nutty Buddy, all soft. My purse is a mess of vanilla and chocolate. "Give me a kiss."

"Mama," she says.

I'm wiping off my hands. "What?"

"I can do it. I can handle it."

"I know you can."

"Like, I mean *alone*. It'll be fine."

I have to shut my mouth so I don't look the fool.

She stands up, smiling a mix between scared and giggling. She never sees me frozen like this, ever.

"Monique," I say. My throat clogs. "What'd you say?"

"Bye, Mama."

She darts in and her lips smack my cheek. Just as quick she's backing off toward that door. She's in, and she's gone.

I see how she planned it like this, drop the bomb and then run.

After all I . . .

Well now.

Doing things her own damn way and no other. Just like me. You try and stop her.

The breeze cuts into me, cooling my sweat, and Mama's right above, laughing her way through a rendition of "Too Close to Heaven." I know down deep my baby don't float, wander, or roam. She's a strong sapling, the start of an acacia tree, planted in somebody's brand-new garden I don't recognize. Some places she's bending, branches straying just like her mama, but that's all right. Sometimes you got to get a little lost on the way to being free.

PARADIS MARTHA SERPAS

The land's so flat you can see yesterday
and the years before that. A future
imperceptible behind haze, vespers,
and an oblong sun burning away.

Lacquered greens, virescent, olive, jade,
emerald. Bold brown bark and gray
moss stack up like mile posts,
proof of a coming providence.

The sky should always disappear
on its own, no hills or buildings blocking
its dominance. Spikes of St. Augustine
clasp our feet: There is only *here*,

and then the up, ahead, and behind called *there*.
More real than time, it holds us, the portent air.

NOW HILL MARTHA SERPAS

/

See the shadow on the hill, that's now,
and the tall trees in dusky light
on the other side, that must be

where you are: in a future
where strong things keep growing.
Smoke fills my lungs then

dissolves in cold air.
Neither can I hold
a plaited river singing to my ears.

EPITHALAMIA MARTHA SERPAS

I.

You will forget this day

as you must

so that later

after the indiscretion or slight

your words will burn

the back of your mortal throat

and you will remember

that you must not vow

what you cannot keep

but take up your intent again

with all your mind and soul

carry it with you and

as Kierkegaard writes

presuppose love

II.

A cleaning woman will gather

the pieces of glass

as if restoring the Temple

No one sees her witness

Her hands are your life

spent picking up

what is shattered

and what you did not break

III.

Two women: one a statue

he cannot touch   the other

holding a rose

This morning she held

his waist and turning her face

he saw her neck flush

The statue's face is a still lake

whose surface he cannot break

The soprano finishes the hymn

and he forgets his place

awed by his imperfection

the self-hatred through which

he honors this girl   the pride

through which he claims this bride

THE PUZZLE OF NAMES MARC HARSHMAN

Inside the closet was where the stars drew nearest. Here he could close his eyes, reach up, and pluck them, one by one, and fill his pockets. The roses dying in the pewter vase on the table had created a kind of leaf fall. There was a sad name waiting to be spelled with their limpid characters there in mother's kitchen. He hated these lessons. And the screaming when the bills came. There were windows but he rarely thought about them. He had seen beyond the brick walls a patch of grass that simmered like lava in the summer and hid under snow in winter, shy in its ugliness. The windows didn't open. Only the door opened, once in the morning and again in the evening. He didn't look but he did like the feel of the wind that would rush inside then, unbidden and free. It would be good to be a door. Or the wind. Or a star. Would someone want to collect him, lay him gently inside their pocket, and work out the puzzle of his name? Perhaps they would join his to all those others bright shining as the sun? And there would be no doors, and the windows would all open.

CANDLEMAS MARC HARSHMAN

What is there to see beyond that window?
The steep hillside anchored with hemlock and oak
    holds its shadows close.
No one comes down from there.
The litter of autumn's coppery leaves
    now scalloped with pools of grainy snow
    will be unruffled this night by any footfall.
And where the wind sings
    its raspy, old man's cough,
    there will be no echo after,
    only the evening's growing stillness.
But he is looking, as if there were someone.
    Three quiet strangers?
    A bright boy with new boots?
    A girl, perhaps, known
    when the trees were younger?
He looks as if there were the certainty of an arrival.
He looks deeply, steadily,
    the very quilt of fragile stars
    slowly flickering on overhead
    trembles under such a gaze
    as if, disturbed by such a longing,
        they might ignite the heavens.

WAITING RYAN GRAUDIN

Gonorrhea, syphilis, chlamydia, warts. One by one the slides of fleshy pink and orange photos flashed across the white screen. Some of the girls in the room gasped, others groaned, about half looked away.

The woman at the front of the room grimaced, her wispy blond hair brushing against her high cheekbones. There was no hint of enjoyment or sadistic pleasure in her glance. The knuckles on her fingers glared white as she wrapped them around the silver remote. She pointed toward the wall, where a glowing red vagina laced with growths sneered at the crowd of high school girls.

"Genital warts can be spread through direct skin-to-skin contact during sex. As you might be able to imagine, they are very painful and impossible to fully eliminate. Sometimes they can be frozen or burned off—but there is always a possibility of their returning. Once you catch them, it's for life."

I shifted in my chair, suddenly conscious of its cold metal surface beneath my legs. I tried not to imagine what they would feel like, burning forever between my thighs with no relief. I could see other girls squirming, trying not to stare too long at the bold, flaming image that towered in front of us all.

"Condoms can help," the woman continued, "but they are not foolproof. In fact, the only way to be completely safe from these diseases is abstinence until marriage."

I looked down at the floor, unable to stare at the scene any longer. I was thankful that I had waited eighteen years, yet doubts began to gnaw in my mind. *But what if your husband has it?* I wondered. *What good would waiting do then?*

* * *

An hour later, another speaker stood in front of the room. In his pale hands he held two pieces of construction paper, red in the left hand, green in the right, their sides glistening with glue-stick residue.

"This is what happens when two unmarried people have sex. It may seem innocent and fun—" He paused, bringing the two pieces together with a resounding thud, "But when all is said and done, it really just hurts them. Because they aren't committed, they eventually split apart."

Slowly, he tugged the green paper away from the red. Crimson chunks clung to the green surface, leaving fiber pits in its red companion.

"When you have sex with someone, you give that person a piece of you and if they leave, that piece of you is gone forever." His voice held a grave tone that sent goose bumps to my arms.

I looked down at my whole, pitless body. It was something special, I knew. By their senior year of high school, most girls I knew had doled out parts of themselves to their sweethearts or on drunken one night stands. I hadn't even been kissed. The closest I had come to a man's touch was a collision in ultimate Frisbee or an innocent side hug with some of the boys in my youth group. I was about as unspoiled as they come.

Part of this was due to a lack of opportunity. Every crush, every love interest in my young adolescent career, had been a miserable, fruitless venture. They either ran their course, dying out in a non-regrettable fashion, or they blew up in my face, leaving me to several weepy nights and chocolate binges. Still, these disasters left me a strong, firm, pitless piece of construction paper.

Ever since I discovered the existence of sex, I knew I wanted to save it. I understood its sacred properties even when I sat in that vast Myrtle Beach parking lot, my hands gripping the gray seat belt tightly as I stared at the cassette player. The shocking information that had emitted from the car stereo was scrambling through my brain, unlocking thirteen years worth of countless puzzles, questions, and observations.

"So," my mom began, leaning back and drumming her hands on the steering wheel, "now you know. Feel free to ask questions."

I glanced at her blankly. Questions? Where to begin? There was so much information this James Dobson tape hadn't provided a breathless pubescent. I drilled her. Questions I now realize as awkward or excessive flooded from my curious mouth: "Do you have to be completely naked? How many times a week do you do it? Where do you do it?" I began to wonder what it was like, how it was done, who I would do it with.

Only one faceless man filled the last slot. It was my husband-to-be, mysterious and unknown, an abstract to be longed for and dreamed about for countless future years.

***

As I grew older, a fear grew inside of me. What if I wasn't able to wait? What if some lustful man asked me to his bed and I was unable to say no? This question kept me awake at night, sitting in a nest of moss green sheets, clutching my pillow and rehearsing the elusive scene. I tried saying "No!" in several tones, at several volumes. I tried to imagine what it would be like to throw my will against my hormones. At the time the struggle seemed brutal. I feared that, despite myself, the animal would win—and instead of one faceless man there would be many, rows and rows of them, outnumbering the warts I would catch.

I was nineteen when I started dating. I found that the struggle wasn't as desperate as I had feared it might be. Holding hands did not send me into a crazed frenzy, a stroke of the hair or the brush of a cheek did not force me into a heated make-out session. I even decided to save my first kiss, falling for the romantic idea that I would reserve the privilege for my fiancé.

Dating was still nice: sitting on a couch in the dead of night, the blue light of the television screen illuminating the room. I loved to stroke his hair, to brush his cheek, to trace his lips with my finger. The exploration was new. It was intimate. We poured out words and emotions with our eyes.

But we could only explore so far. We came to a point where the trail was barred, a No Trespassing sign plastered against the slender body of a pine tree. New land was not open to us, so we lingered in old territory. Sometimes striding impatiently, sometimes languishing, sometimes lunging at the gate.

"Okay, guys, I have a question." Gabrielle stood up from the booth, brushing crumbs of popcorn shrimp away from her hostess uniform. "How old were you when you lost your virginity?"

I sighed and glanced down at my grilled chicken salad. Lunch break at Bubba Gump was always an interesting affair. It was common knowledge that more than half of the restaurant workers had "shared the love" with each other. In fact, it wasn't unusual to find waitresses comparing the number of venereal diseases they had obtained.

How old? Answers popped up from the nearby tables. Seventeen. Fifteen. One guy held out until twenty-four. It was my turn.

"I'm actually still a virgin," I said.

I was proud of the fact; I had fought much raging libido for the status. My boyfriend of four months was a virgin as well. Our rigid guidelines and personal convictions had served us well on dimly lit nights in his apartment. We never did more than light snuggling.

There was a brief silence. One of the waitresses broke in, "Wow, that's actually really cool." There were some nods of agreement.

I shrugged.

Word traveled fast. I was a sensation, especially among the male servers. My boyfriend, David, was a server. He regaled me with slightly humorous accounts of his encounters with the gossip.

"So when you were walking away from Russell and me the other day, Russell turned to me and whispered, 'Hey, man. Did you know she's a virgin? Isn't that hot?' When I told him that you were my girlfriend, he got slightly embarrassed."

I laughed, yet my insides bristled at the thought of my coworker's fantasies. Inevitably they would exist, but I would have preferred not to be aware of them.

"I LIKE YOU TOO MUCH."

It's a strange thing for a boyfriend to say, but David said it every so often and I knew what was coming next.

"I think about sex too much when I'm around you. It's not good."

I sighed, knowing what this meant. It meant another few weeks of our "physical fast," where our contact was limited simply to hand-holding and farewell hugs. It was a good discipline to have for two young adults seeking abstinence, but the animal inside me always snarled a bit selfishly at being deprived of what little physical affection it received.

David continued, "It would probably be best if we went on a physical fast, you know, to clear our heads."

He was right. I knew I was lucky to have a boyfriend who actually took the offense in our quest for sexual purity. God had blessed me with a man who was content to sit on a couch and stroke my hair—a man who never even considered putting pressure on me. All of those nights spent rehearsing No! had been in vain. I never needed to use it for him.

STILL, I OFTEN GROW TIRED OF THE STRUGGLE, venting my frustrations with God in my journal: *Dear God, I want to get married and have sex NOW. Arg. Damn school. Damn selfish lusts. Damn sex drive.*

Perhaps it's not my best prayer, but it's one of my more honest ones.

I know that one day, the waiting will be worth it. I will never regret passing up summer flings and one-night stands with frat boys. I will never wish I had given it away at the first possible chance. I won't even regret the year and a half of chastity I have spent so far with David.

When the gate opens and the NO TRESPASSING sign falls, I will eagerly proceed. There will be no danger, no fear of warts or ill-timed babies. Just some crazy journey with the man I have pledged my life to.

I can't wait. But I will.

A LENTEN MEDITATION GINA MARIE MAMMANO V.

We seek among the flowers
the bloodbloom of martyrs,
the deepest red we can find;
we want to taste the sacrifice
on our lips, make mouth
crimson on their behalf,
feel we have red in us as well.
Wish that life can pool in
places and rain puddles of
little deaths can characterize
our little lives.
But what about the lily?
The white cream cup that is
untouched by the drip drip
of human sorrow, the pale
beauty that can make
lips smell clean? What
about the living sacrifice?
The terrifying magic of a
flower well-bloomed.

WHISTLER SHANNA POWLUS WHEELER

I married a whistler of old hymns.
Tonight "Love Lifted Me"
rings through the hallway. The cat's black-tipped ears
swivel on the chorus—each high *love*
and the notes tumbling after.
    The melody repeats like the tide
but does not weary me, the listener
who cannot whistle, who scrubs dishes
while the whistler carries buckets of coal
from garage to stove.
    This winter night, what cheer
his o-ringed lips offer me;
his embouchure and clear trill lift me
from work-day billows, all my frothy fears
like a daily grace, a hand
like His hand.

TWO OF EVERY KIND LYNN DOMINA

First she thought the menagerie
simply another of his enthusiasms, fervent,
bizarre, short-lived. The guinea fowl
satisfied themselves with corn he fed
his speckled hens. Three days later, he carted home
a pair of Rhode Island reds and two long-billed parrots
she'd never seen the likes of. He must have bartered
some fine cloth or heavy jewel; yet she found nothing
missing. A good year passed

before he heaved those cubs against her loom.
Two he called polar bear, the others red fox.
By then, she'd given up
her one rule—no animals inside—
so long as he built that monstrosity
far from her fig grove, back where extra shade
could harm nothing. While heavy clouds

stalled above their town, she christened
African mammals, fresh-water fish. The emperor penguins
she called after her own grandparents.
The best name of all
she saved for the white-tailed deer, her belly
roiling with young. The woman
led the deer aboard, tamped down a bed of straw,
waited through thunder as they pitched starboard,
aft. Both fawns
tottered toward the woman, nuzzled her palms
until she recognized each
as female, her husband's perfectly correspondent world
already assuredly undone.

FIRST MORNING IN HEAVEN LYNN DOMINA

Clover lifts slightly, stills, the breeze a brief
silent whiff. You never knew you'd longed
so for silence. Chipmunks here
scatter quietly; field mice
nibble softened seeds. You remember reading
how giraffes only seem mute to human ears;
one female suddenly nuzzles
the top of your head, tongues
a single strawberry from your plate. You'd waited months,
swimming in Squam Lake, to hear a loon cry
until one did cry off to the north, unmistakable as people said.
Your delight fills you again; one cries here, too,
beyond sight. You recall
leafy sea dragons, the most astonishingly bizarre creatures
you ever beheld, as twigs nudge lily pads across the pond,
tousled leaves dipping beneath ripples. They survive
in the New England Aquarium
and along Australia's southern coast,
another place you still plan to visit, if only to listen
for a kookaburra's raucous laughter,
pocket a dropped tail feather, like this one,
left by the plump male who springs from your porch swing now.
Once you saw a blue heron lift itself from shallows;
once you saw a bobcat
amble across your road. Impossible, visions
out of time. Yet you saw
once and see again.

ANTIQUE SHOP LYNN DOMINA

On my way out, I unlatch
a small cabinet, ornate crosses
nailed to each panel. The proprietor
hurries to reveal why priests
owned such things. I finger
the faded stole, crusted candle, crucifix, the tarnished pyx.

Last rites they called it

before it became the sacrament
of the sick. My friend lay dying,
so ravaged that her priest
could be forgiven
for reciting prayers
for the dead. She arched her neck
until he paged, mortified,
to those prayers for the dying and then she stopped
breathing. Water, chrism

a blessing chanted
in English and Latin, *In paradisum
deducant te angeli.* Of course I believe
angels welcomed her to paradise,
even as I doubt
the reality of angels.

I believe in blessing.

I want the stole, the pyx, the priest's whole cabinet.
He's surely in heaven now, sighing

at my temptation. I confess
I'm slightly simoniac,
more than slightly,
though what I want is not the cross
nor the hand that held this stole
laid on me, but the breath,

the last one, its calm urgency,
but then another, another.

APOSTATE'S CHALLENGE LYNN DOMINA

I dreamed my gluttony would nauseate death.
I dreamed I shook with hunger and so ate death.

The invitation urges us to dress as our favorite phobia.
I choose a king cobra, you a black rat. No one aims to impersonate death.

Blood courses through my capillaries faster than Israelites
through the Red Sea, but not fast enough to exsanguinate death.

We watch the grieving mother claw her scalp, gouge her face,
tearing her own flesh as though she wishes to lacerate death.

Bury me deep but visit me often. Scatter someone else's ashes
in the mountains, across the lake—we'll never immolate death.

You can't create for me a more compelling creature than Satan
looming from fire, alive, triumphant over that reprobate, death.

In every culture, shame trumps honor. We slit our wrists;
they plunge swords into their bellies. Does either gesture eviscerate death?

My name suggests a lady to some lord. Who
could lord it over mortality, dominate death?

MARRIAGE AFTER WAR: A FRUITFUL QUESTION NATASHA LYNN HELLER

What now?
We look at each other
across the table at Old Chicago,
each asking ourselves that question,
inside.
It boils like jelly
on the stove,
sour, threatening to spill over,
and tasting of
old apricots.

You have been to war,
sand under eyelids,
skin-biting metals,
so far from me I seemed
like dream-fluff,
slipping through the fingers
of your mind,
unsatisfying,
like describing an apple
to a man who's
never eaten.

I have fought the quiet battles,
been cut by wicked blades that
sink all the deeper
for not being seen.
Crying that perfect prayer
of tears and no words,
I woke mornings

MARRIAGE AFTER WAR: A FRUITFUL QUESTION

to feel as if
God Himself
stroked my hair
while I slept,
watching me miss you
in the furrows of my brow,
like cracks in a
sun-split melon.

We have had that first love-making,
back at the hotel,
each kiss a small explosion,
like pomegranate seeds
bursting their juice in our mouths,
ripe touches on our bruised skins
as we devoured each other
with our hands,
so long-empty.

The poor waitress will be lucky
if we remembered a tip tonight.
I stumble over chair legs in my heels,
following you,
still used to leading.
When I catch up I will
lock my arm into yours
and throw away the key,
my hip fitting spoon-snug
against you as we walk
the rough-ice streets.

I've heard there's another room
around here somewhere,
windows shattering,
filling, as it is,
with a star-shaped fruit

that tastes of light.
They say when we try it,
(and that's soon)
our eyes will never
stop their shining.

MEMORIAL DAY DEANNA HERSHISER

Coast

Windows open to salt-bit breezes, we drive uphill at the west end of town. My husband, Tim, steers us toward the beach road.

We're here, the Friday of Memorial Day weekend, because our son needs to rendezvous with his Marine Biology class at an Oregon coast tide pool tomorrow morning. We decided to make the two-hour trip from our Willamette Valley home and camp tonight. Tim used to be an engineer for the local TV station—he helped maintain an array of nearby transmitters and towers. As he tells our son stories of gale force storms and equipment failures, I glance at passing landmarks. An unexpected shudder threads up my spine.

Should I have come?

This avenue boasts pizza places, a credit union, and farther on a Wal-Mart that did not exist when we lived here.

The Quick Cash Loans office turns my head. I used to park my car near the building's square profile five afternoons a week, back when it was a 7-Eleven.

Three years after marrying Tim and a while before motherhood, I worked the four to midnight shift by myself. Behind counter and between shelves I assisted customers, sold Big Gulps, checked IDs of guys buying beer who looked early twenties like me. Across town Tim ran master control at the TV station until two in the morning.

Long-buried sensations sputter inside my chest. It's stupid, I decide, and yet driving through this end of town must be the culprit. Ancient emotions rise—I'm willing to give them a nod—but I plan to maintain composure.

Past the city limits our van follows curved lengths of highway nearing the campground. Ocean patches appear. Tim is silent now.

Managing a smile, I reach to pat his knee. "You doing okay?"

"I'm wondering why the oscillator on the digital modulator is still unstable and keeps causing the frequency to drift. I'll probably have to go in and work on it tomorrow after we get home."

"Oh. Sorry."

"But otherwise I'm fine."

That's my techno guy.

Long Ago

He's been in my life, basically, forever. When we tell friends our parents all knew each other before we were born, eyebrows raise. Arranged marriage?

Hardly. Growing up I thought of Tim as that older boy whose family came to our house in Tacoma, Washington, every few summers to visit. Our parents sat on kitchen chairs on the patio, sipping juice and discussing life in the ministry. Ignoring me, Tim took apart and swabbed with alcohol our crackling stereo speakers. He fixed Mom's cassette recorder and rewired our doorbell.

In 1977 I turned seventeen and suspected Tim considered me differently. *A long time ago in a galaxy far, far away* emblazoned movie screens that summer. Tim asked me to ride in his '66 Ford, a cool car my brothers dubbed the Millennium Falcon. I went along, because regarding relationships I spoke to myself in terms Darth Vader might have used, "Your training is now complete." I assumed the co-pilot's seat and tucked one leg beneath the other.

Tim said, "You should fasten your seatbelt."

"I do when I'm driving," I said.

Tim drove without mentioning it again. He handed me a map detailing the Milton-Fife area. "I noticed a couple trailer parks around there," he said, pointing. "See which way we turn after the exit."

The two of us zipped north on I-5.

"It's thirty miles from your house to where I work now," Tim said. "So I'd like to live in my travel trailer someplace in between."

"Oh?" I glanced at him sideways.

Tim grinned. "Since your mom always needs someone to pick you up after work."

Mom had asked him to fetch me a few times from my aunt's jewelry shop downtown, after he'd shown up on a Friday or Saturday evening before supper. I hadn't minded seeing his face at the end of several boring hours behind the cash register.

We exited the freeway and took a winding road that turned out to be wrong.

"So when you said go right you meant we should turn left?" Tim said.

"Hmm. Maybe that was it," I said, spreading and rotating the map again.

Tim's morning-blue eyes twinkled. He didn't seem to mind being lost with me.

Finally we arrived at the Firs Mobile Park of West Milton, and Tim met the park owner, a gray-haired gentleman.

"That the missus?" he asked Tim, pointing to where I waited in the car.

"Uh, no," Tim said.

"Girlfriend?"

"Well, no."

"Sister?"

"No. Sort of a cousin."

We laughed all the way back to my house. Tim had signed papers and would move his trailer to a space rimmed by ancient spruce. That autumn Tim would ask me out. We two children of preacher men would begin navigating our sexuality on a planet more crazed and shadowed than the past few generations had foreseen.

By the next time I hopped in the Falcon for a ride with Tim, a Triple-A sticker on his glove box proclaimed FASTEN SAFETY BELT.

I buckled.

I decided, soon after Tim asked me, that marriage looked a proposition worthy of our emotions and our heritage. With both our fathers we stood at the front of the church, plenty more pastors looking on and blessing us, never imagining I would one day jump ship.

GLIMPSE

We pull into the campground, set up our tent, and fix supper. Then we drive to a sheltered, rock-strewn beach where sunset's blush adorns dark veils beyond the surf.

Tim and our son head over before nightfall toward looming cliffs to peer inside a cave. I can't decide which direction to stroll along the firm sand.

To my left teenagers cluster near a parked car; two guys shout and, laughing, begin a light scuffle. I choose a meandering route to the right. A longing to kick off shoes conflicts with fear of losing them in twilight's dimness. I pause, awkward.

Scanning gentle waves that wash into the cove, I catch a glimpse of something. A small round shape bobs between crests—the ebony head of a sea lion.

Smoothly it disappears. I strain to find it, but shadows and faint glimmers trick my eyes. Did I really see it? Yes. The sea lion is there, closer to shore and unmistakable.

I imagine a female—she watches me and wonders what makes a land creature stand silent in descending gloom. Perhaps the sea lion is a mother who hunts salmon for her children. Or maybe my fanciful kinship is with a younger ocean adult, away from her mate, seeking bearings.

Shark Gills

On an October afternoon in 1982 I wheeled out the floor mop bucket at 7-Eleven, my smock-covered torso bent to the task. My wedding ring adorned the hand steadying the wringer.

Video game sentinels bleeped in their corner. The glass front door's automatic ding announced an entrant. I looked up to see a familiar customer towering, grinning. I blushed.

"Busy today, huh?"

"Well, no. Just mopping." Brilliant, I thought.

"I'll take my Camel straights, if you can spare the time." His hair, lighter than Tim's, brushed his blue jacket's collar.

As I hurried behind the counter for BJ's cigarettes more customers came in. BJ quipped, "Hey, Ditzy, you getting that divorce yet?"

"What? No."

He liked to tease, to catch me off-guard. Often BJ showed up several times during my shifts to buy odds and ends or play Ms. Pac-Man. "I'm a laid-off longshoreman," he'd confided once, leaning against the Slurpee machine while I restocked cups.

Counting his change, I attempted to return BJ's banter. My tongue's never been a smooth dancer; often it trips whole routines, causing awkward pauses. I fumbled and sensed my cheeks coloring more.

BJ shook his head, flashed his smile. "Later, Ditzy," he said.

In three years with Tim I hadn't let my attention stray to another man. Once a memory of an old boyfriend briefly invaded a dream, shaking me awake. I'd tucked it firmly inside a back closet of my mind.

Now I found myself watching for BJ's car to again halt in front of the dinging door, its vents on the front fenders like a shark's gills.

After work I waited at home for Tim, tunes pulsing through our dim rooms from my favorite Journey album, *Escape*. When he arrived, as had become Tim's habit, he went to his collection of radios—a CB base station and some others—through which he often traded stories with truckers and old men on wireless sets till not long before dawn.

"I wish you were as eager to see me as those gadgets," I said from his workroom doorway.

Tim's eyes shone with excitement. "I've found this neat bunch of people," he said. "They're on every night."

I yawned. "I bought a bag of candy at work for the Trick-or-Treaters."

"Not this soon," Tim said, smirking. "You'll eat every piece by tomorrow. We'll have nothing to give those poor little kids."

"I don't eat that much candy! Why do you talk like I'm out of control, or fat, or . . . ?"

Tim grinned. "I don't think you're too fat."

I whirled away, stomping.

"You're just so much fun to tease."

Drifting off in our waterbed, I heard one scratching voice ask Tim, "You got a wife waitin' in the other room? I wouldn't stay on air too long."

"Oh, she's sleeping," Tim replied.

Near Christmas they replaced the Donkey Kong video game at 7-Eleven with a new one called Dig Dug.

As I breezed between store shelves, the cooler stocked and my shift finally over, BJ slid quarters into the new machine. When I stepped out of the office with sweater and purse, he glanced up at me.

"Stupid game," he remarked.

"How do you play?" I asked.

"Come here and I'll show you."

BJ stood behind me. "Your turn first," he said. His fingers guided my hand. "There. Make the digger guy drop that rock on the monster." While I tried to accomplish the task, BJ's thumb nudged my wedding band.

I focused halfway on the thrumming game. Just learning something new, I said to myself. No sense going home until Tim's done at the station.

Another regular, Cal, a wiry man who knew the storeowner, came in around one. Cal got coffee and chatted with the burly young guy who worked graveyard. "Hey there, Dee," he said to me with a nod.

"I'd better head home," I said, next to BJ, watching him get close to Dig Dug's fifth level.

"Damn!" BJ exclaimed, swatting the joystick control. "Oh, sorry, Ditzy. Later."

By January I had to tell myself, driving west through town to the store, everything was under control. Anything's possible. But nothing's inevitable.

I tried to talk to Tim. At home on our waterbed watching *Dr. Who*, I organized words and constructed vague questions.

"Would you dive into a pool you know might be empty?" I asked close to my husband's shoulder. Tim remained engrossed in the show.

"What do you think it's really like on the dark side?"

Tim glanced my way. "Huh?"

He just totally doesn't get me, I thought.

One February evening I paced behind the 7-Eleven counter. When BJ came in I slipped him a folded paper. On it were words, penned to suit, I hoped, a relationship blooming. They spoke my fantasy of strolls near the ocean, getting to know one another, the longings of love.

He read it. "What's this bullshit?" he said low.

I swallowed.

"You got a pen?" He scribbled something. "I can meet you at this motel." His smile spoke desire, and my own answered in kind.

Later I met him there. Just the one night. Afterward BJ drove away in his shark-faced car.

Low Tide

I wander the shore. My sea lion companion is gone.

Tim and our son stride up. "That's a pretty deep crevice between the rocks," he says about the cave they ventured into. My husband's face seems to shine in the gloaming.

I throw my arms around Tim's chest and hold tight, promising both of them s'mores when we reach camp. My husband feels solid, alive, and his features appear calm. It's never been easy looking at him to discern pain's residue.

If men and women with a history somehow magically developed telepathic abilities, I would toss Tim a question:

Are you thinking about Memorial Day weekend, 1983?

Next morning, an hour past sunrise, I scoot my chair close to Tim's steady campfire. Savoring a bowl of oatmeal, I sip hot cocoa and watch sun-swords cast themselves between fir boughs.

Tim has taken our son to meet up with classmates and teacher on a beach exposed by an ultra low tide.

I asked the guys if they minded my staying behind. Lazy, perhaps, but I've decided I'll accept these rare moments to linger and reflect.

My Choice

After that winter night with BJ I recognized two things. Because God doesn't miss a whisper I was done for, my marriage wrecked. Sooner or later the Creator would destroy me. Also, I disgusted myself. Though somehow certain after he drove off that BJ would never return, I still wanted him.

Whether or not I imagined maintaining a sophisticated pose around Tim, I don't recall. But the next kiss from my husband, a day or two later, dislodged my secret.

"I've wronged you," I told Tim, chin to my collar. "In the worst way."

He shuddered as he sought composure. No tools at his workbench could mend this.

Silent, I slipped out the door.

I drove to a bluff near the ocean and stared at the sunset sky. Beyond those tinted clouds the God I'd grown up with sat, judging me. *This you can never undo.* He who sent his word to mankind had made sure I got an earful each Sunday. Now I'd betrayed everything I'd thought and said growing up.

I didn't know what to do except go back to our place.

The next weeks we stayed together, stepping around each other. His days off Tim traveled two hours to the valley. Up and down I-5 he sought a job to ferry us inland. When he returned he spent whole nights organizing my haphazard linen closet and waxing the utility room floor.

At work I watched in vain outside the storefront for BJ's car. Tulips opened beside the credit union across the street, the sky darkened later each evening.

One busy night BJ pulled in. Behind the counter I held my breath while the customer ahead of him finished. Then I ventured a smile.

A woman with stringy hair stepped up as he asked for his Camels. "You forgot the milk," she said to him, holding forth a gallon.

"Damn it, woman," he replied. "Get in the car."

I took his money and turned away. As the door dinged I slammed the cash register closed.

Next morning I glanced sidelong at Tim as he buttered toast. Wishing to loosen the set of his jaw I asked softly, "How are you?"

Tim looked up. "How soon can you quit 7-Eleven?" His words were granite. "I heard back from Portland a week ago, and I'll start training at KPTV next Monday."

"But—so soon?"

"There's a hotel right across the street, until I can find us a place to rent."

"I'll have to give notice. They'll have to get someone else. It might take a while." My heart thudded. I hadn't wanted to consider we'd really move away.

The first of May Tim started running camera at KPTV. I stayed behind at our place to pack and to finish at 7-Eleven.

A bizarre sensation enveloped me. I felt as though I viewed someone else, a woman on a movie screen, acting out these moments in my history.

Evenings off the woman danced alone in my room to records, my soundtrack. I watched her obsess over a man who drove a shark car and smoked Camels.

"Hey, Dee, how you doing?" Cal, the wiry customer who was friends with my boss, waited across the counter at 7-Eleven to pay for coffee. "You need to talk to someone?"

"Oh, not really."

"I noticed you haven't played Dig Dug for a while."

"No."

"I'll be here when you get done tonight. Maybe help you fill the cooler."

"Thanks."

With Tim away, I began spending time most nights after work with Cal. We took walks through town in the tangy air. "Tell me something," he'd say. He asked questions about who I was. What I thought of life and death and religion.

"I'm sure God is mad at me," I told him one night. "I felt like this before I got married, when Tim and I nearly went all the way." I chuckled at the irony.

"But now," I said, "I just have to continue and stay married. To do what's right."

"If you think so," Cal said. "You seem real unhappy to me, though. Why don't we go for a drive?"

Stars blinked at us through amorphous clouds. The beach was sheltered.

"Dee," Cal said. "Come here. Let's quit fooling—I want you." A thrill pricked my scalp.

I asked him, "Can we kiss and not tell?"

But I told Tim. We met mid-month, midway between coastline and city. "I can't live with you in Portland," I said. "I've made my choice."

Back at our place I began separating my unruly stuff from Tim's. I set my wedding ring in a box in a drawer.

For a week or two I allowed the movie me to indulge in a montage, its soundtrack a carefree pop tune. With her new man, Cal, she picnicked, hiked, and went fishing by day. Late nights they hung out in various entertainment spots and at the homes of some of his friends.

The people she met related their stories of dealing with an ex, of getting on with life's details. They drank, smoked, and laughed on cue.

I began staying mainly at Cal's, a tiny house with dilapidated vehicles in the yard. A vague plan emerged between us to move my boxes over from the place Tim and I were vacating.

My fix-it husband obtained a do-it-yourself divorce kit. He arranged to see me on the coast, bringing the papers the Saturday of Memorial Day weekend. By the time he showed up on our doorstep Tim was drunk.

"I wanted to tell you I've been praying," he said, missing the chair I offered and thudding on the floor.

Despite a heavy heart, I nearly laughed. I'd never seen him this way, definitely full of the spirit. I sat beside him.

Tim continued. "I said to God, why has this happened? And you know something?"

"What?"

"I realized I don't want to lose you. I want our marriage."

Tim went on expressing emotions. He told me he longed to rebuild our life, to start again.

"I ordered the divorce kit, but it's a last resort. I don't want a lawyer involved; they expect the process to divide us, so they can get paid. I want this to end in us finding a way back together."

I glanced past Tim. Through the workroom door his radios sat silent, unused for many weeks.

"I've been unfaithful to you," I said. I remembered the hardness in his voice the day he'd announced we were moving.

"But," Tim said, "I broke my vow to cherish you. I haven't cherished you the way I should've." He stood. "Excuse me."

Tim ran for the bathroom and remained there a long time.

I opened a window to the evening breeze. My brain felt linty. All I could think about was Tim saying, before we married, how glad he was I had never been sullied by wild living or another man.

It's way too late, I thought. I reached for a pen and signed the divorce papers.

Later as he stood pale before me I handed them to Tim. "I'm sorry," I said. "I don't know what I feel anymore."

"Could we at least try praying together?"

I stepped back. "What good would that do?" The words landed dully between us.

"Why not? We've tried everything else."

"But, damn it." I raised my purse and threw it on the table. Keys and Kleenex spilled. "I am so angry with God!" My outburst surprised us both.

We stood there.

"Okay," I said.

Knees on linoleum. Hands clasped. Tim's tears. Then mine. We prayed in halting voices. Afterward we blew our noses.

Somewhere in the neighborhood a child laughed, in the night where scents of barbeques lingered.

I'd always heard God blessed, ordained, created marriage. I'd been focused on a hurricane, the destruction my instincts told me I deserved.

Was God somehow for us, despite everything?

Tim drove to Portland; I made a phone call then went to 7-Eleven.

Cal stood talking, blowing on his coffee.

"Dee? What's going on?"

"I'm heading out of town, to stay with my parents," I said. "I just need to get far from this place so I can think."

"All right," he said. I slipped into my car while he walked to his.

As I drove away I glimpsed him in the rearview mirror for the last time.

Sheltered

Above our campsite a ceiling of heavy clouds builds. Soon, accompanied by chilled breezes, water drops. The tent is being pattered, and I move beneath its cover.

Memories could keep me absorbed for hours, but I figure the guys will head back in a bit. Besides, I'd rather not dwell on the years when, during bad days with Tim, I grasped at shirttails of imagining one last rendezvous with Cal. I've decided God never says the past gets flushed away. Faded movie endings remain frozen behind the credits on screen.

Standing in Twilight

In Tacoma in June of 1983 I spent days alone on my childhood bed, reading, thinking, writing to Tim. "I don't expect anything from you," I wrote. "I'll take things slowly, maybe look for a job. See what comes next."

I imagined we'd start over, meeting someplace, making tentative dates to wander flower gardens and museums. As it turned out, I got the flu.

My mom fixed chicken soup. Finally my temperature lowered. My hair a frizz mountain, I rose weakly onto an elbow when someone knocked at the bedroom door. "Come in," I said.

It was Tim. "I'd like to bring you home," he said.

I knew then that I wanted to go with him.

In seasons to come I fretted and whined and rejoiced and laughed and gave birth and went to church. I scheduled regular prayer sessions between Tim and me, but those languished beneath mundane skies.

Despite our best intentions, everydayness brought us more of ourselves. His wit sliced me; my emotions flummoxed him. And yet brighter realities showed up, too—Tim would take me in his arms when kids left the house for an afternoon; I'd get us lost on back roads in the still-cool Millennium Falcon.

I puzzled over our story's implications. I tried crusading for the rebinding and health of every marriage. One friend clung to my assurances regarding her philanderous husband.

While church folk vowed to pray him back to Jesus, I spooned her my confidence in God's desire to rescue them. Months later they divorced.

Life began to illuminate for me different patterns and questions regarding faith. Did I define God as rigid, attired in traditional regulation? Did God expect me to hand in forms with every blank completed, flawless?

I assumed that after repenting I'd be plunked beside an apple tree, while a booming voice commanded, *Get it right this time, woman; don't sample the fruit, no matter what that other guy tells you.*

Instead, in undeserved gifts I found a purpose and reason for wide-eyed, deliberate living. I couldn't have predicted the extent to which mercy would intrigue me, like a glimpse between breakers of someone standing in twilight on firm sand.

Valley

At noon Tim and our son return and we navigate breaking soggy camp. Our boy says he barely noticed getting wet during his eventful morning around pungent tide pools brimming with sea stars and anemones.

"Grab the other side of the tent," Tim tells him, tossing a rag. They stretch the fabric structure flat, wiping and folding.

Releasing tent pole sections, I sigh. "Being here sure brought back memories."

"Yeah," Tim says. "Terminal rain."

After he arranges everything to fit, we pile in the car. My turn to drive. I buckle up and stretch my arms; Tim reaches fast, tickles my ribs, then leans close for a moment.

At the turn beside our cove from last evening I glimpse the squallish, empty ocean in the rearview mirror. East toward the valley, past damp fields and weathered barns lining the highway, I take us home.

AUTHOR BIOS

AN INTRODUCTION TO OUR AUTHORS

STACY BARTON
WHEN I WAS TWELVE
Fiction

These days Stacy is primarily a short story author and playwright. Her debut collection of short stories, *Surviving Nashville*, was released in 2007. Her stories and poetry have appeared in a variety of literary magazines like *Potomac Review*, *Relief*, *Ruminate*, and *Stonework* and her fifth stage play, an adaptation of Dylan Thomas's *A Child's Christmas in Wales*, premiered in Orlando, Florida, last year. In addition to short stories, plays, and poetry, Stacy is the author of a children's picture book and an animated short film. She is currently a freelance scriptwriter for the Disney Company.

JUSTIN RYAN BOYER
AMERICAN DREAM
Poetry

Justin feels like he is in an episode of *Seinfeld* when writing about himself in the third-person. Random creativity, redemption, a good chai, and sincere friendships are some of his favorite things (he doesn't like whiskers on kittens). Naomi, his wife, is the most important person in his life, even if he doesn't realize it all the time. Writing is communal, therapeutic, and prophetic—Justin started a little online writing group to learn more about those avenues (www.silhouettewords.com). He thinks orthodoxy and mystery are essential and hopes to know who he really is before he hits the afterlife.

DAVID BREEDEN
BEING SOMEWHERE
CHAPLAIN NOTES
Poetry

Dr. David Breeden has an MFA from the Writers' Workshop at the University of Iowa, a PhD from the Center for Writers at the University of Southern Mississippi, and a Master of Divinity from Meadville Lombard Theological School. He has published four novels and nine books of poems. He is a Unitarian Universalist minister.

ZACHARY DAVIS
THE PEGASUS LANDING
Fiction

Zachary Davis lives in Oregon's Willamette Valley. He received his bachelor's degree in Liberal Arts from Gutenberg College. Presently, he lives in Portland, Oregon, and works for a small winery.

LYNN DOMINA
ANTIQUE SHOP
APOSTATE'S CHALLENGE
FIRST MORNING IN HEAVEN
TWO OF EVERY KIND
Poetry

AUTHOR BIOS

Lynn Domina is the author of a collection of poetry, *Corporal Works*, and the editor of a collection of essays, *Poets on the Psalms*. Her recent poetry appears in *Prairie Schooner*, *The Southern Review*, *The Green Mountains Review*, and several other periodicals. She currently lives in the western Catskill region of New York.

SHELLY DRANCIK
FACES
Fiction

Shelly Drancik is attaining her MFA from Queens University. She lives in Batavia, Illinois, with her husband and three children. This short-short is her first publication.

MIKE DURAN
THE ARK
Editor's Choice in Creative Nonfiction

Mike's stories have appeared in *Relief*, *Coach's Midnight Diner*, *Fear and Trembling*, *Forgotten Worlds*, *Alienskin*, *Infuze Magazine*, and *Dragons, Knights, and Angels*, with articles in *The Matthew's House Project*, *Relevant Magazine* and *316 Journal*. Mike is currently part of the editorial team for the *Midnight Diner's* second edition and contributes monthly commentary at Novel Journey. He and his wife Lisa live in Southern California, where they have raised four children. You can visit him at www.mikeduran.com.

RYAN GRAUDIN
WAITING
Creative Nonfiction

Although she has been struck with a hopeless case of wanderlust, Ryan remains for a twenty-second year in her hometown of Charleston, South Carolina, as she finishes her BA in English at the College of Charleston. Since the writing of this essay her wonderful boyfriend David proposed and she said yes. They got married on May 17, 2008, and have been living the newlywed dream (And yes, it is worth the wait!).

MELANIE HANEY
THE LAST THING BEFORE DIRT
Editor's Choice in Fiction

Melanie Haney lives in the woods of Southern New Hampshire with her husband and two small children. She holds an MFA from Lesley University and was the winner of the 2006 Family Circle Fiction Competition and the 2007 Ann Arbor Book Festival Short Story Competition. Her work has appeared or is forthcoming in *Family Circle Magazine*, *Quality Women's Fiction*, *Eureka Literary Magazine*, *Fifth Wednesday Journal*, *elimae*, *The Summerset Review*, and more. She can be found online at http://melaniehaney.blogspot.com

AUTHOR BIOS

MARC HARSHMAN
CANDLEMAS
THE PUZZLE OF NAMES
Poetry

Raised in rural Indiana, Marc Harshman has lived his adult life in West Virginia where, for many years, he was a grade school teacher. Periodical publication of his poems include *The Georgia Review*, *Rock & Sling*, *Tusculum Review*, *Shenandoah*, and *The Progressive*. He is the author of three chapbooks of poetry including most recently *Local Journeys* (Finishing Line, 2004). He is also the author of eleven children's picture books including *The Storm*, a Smithsonian Notable Book for Children, Parent's Choice Award winner, and Junior Library Guild selection. He holds degrees from Bethany College, Yale Divinity School, and the University of Pittsburgh.

LYN HAWKS
MIDRIFT
Fiction

Lyn Hawks taught high school for several years and now develops curriculum for gifted youth. She is co-author of *The Compassionate Classroom: Lessons that Nurture Wisdom and Empathy* and *Teaching Romeo and Juliet: A Differentiated Approach*. She also writes for *FacultyShack*, an online journal for teachers. She lives in Chapel Hill, North Carolina, with her husband, Greg Hawks, a bluegrass musician, and her orange tabby, Sonny. She is chronicling her writer's journey at www.lynhawks.com

NATASHA LYNN HELLER
MARRIAGE AFTER WAR: A FRUITFUL QUESTION
Poetry

First, Natasha wishes to offer up thanks to the Lord for giving her poems after she had sworn them off. She has a BA in creative writing and has been published in *GreenPrints* and *Critique*. She is currently working on a novel so that she can look mysterious and broody in coffee shops.

DEANNA HERSHISER
MEMORIAL DAY
Creative Nonfiction

Deanna Hershiser writes essays and lives with her engineer husband, Tim, in Eugene, Oregon. Tim listens to her as she processes life for the page, and Deanna watches TV with him whenever there's a new episode of *Dr. Who*.

ED HIGGINS
DAYLIGHT SAVINGS
Poetry

Ed Higgins and his wife and three whippets live on a small farm south of Portland, Oregon, where they remain unrepentant holdovers from the early 70s "back-to-the-land" movement. They raise a small menagerie of chickens, turkeys, ducks, geese, pigs, Jersey cows, Nubian goats, an emu named To & Fro, and a rescued potbelly pig named Odious. He teaches creative writing and literature at George Fox University and his poems and short fiction have appeared in *Monkeybicycle*, *Pindeldyboz*, and *Bellowing Ark*, as well as the online journals *Lily*, *CrossConnect*, *The Centrifugal Eye*, *Mannequin Envy*, and *Red River Review*, among others.

ANN IVERSON
AFTER PAINTING
LOVE
SOLSTICE NEARING
SUNFLOWERS
Poetry

Ann Iverson is the author of *Come Now to the Window*, published by Laurel Poetry Collective in 2003 and *Definite Space* published by Holy Cow! Press in 2007. Her writing has been featured on *The Writer's Almanac* with Garrison Keillor and has appeared or is forthcoming in *The Oklahoma Review*, *Margie: American Journal of Poetry*, *Water-Stone Review*, *Poetry East*, and others. A visual artist, Ann takes interest in the intuitive and cyclical exchanges made between language and image. Her first art exhibit, peaking Image, debuted at the *Undercroft Gallery* in St. Paul. This work portrays the language within image and the image within language. She currently is the Director of Arts and Sciences at Dunwoody College of Technology in Minneapolis. She and her husband live in East Bethel, Minnesota.

JILL NOEL KANDEL
LETTERS HOME FROM SUNSHINE MOUNTAIN
Creative Nonfiction

Jill Noel Kandel grew up in North Dakota listening to prairie stories. She has lived in Zambia, Indonesia, England, and in her husband's native Netherlands. After working abroad for ten years she returned to the U.S. and currently lives with her husband and children in Minnesota. Jill has been published in *Image: A Journal of Arts and Religion*, *Brevity: A Journal of Concise Literary Nonfiction*, and in *Apalachee Review*. This is her second publication in *Relief*.

ELIZA KELLEY
STORY OF A TREE
Poetry

Portrait artist and writer Eliza Kelley teaches Creative Writing, Human Rights Discourse, and American Minority Literature at Buffalo State College in New York. Recent work appears in *Conte*, *Common Sense 2*, and *Tonopah Review*.

AMY LETTER
ON EARTH
Creative Nonfiction

Amy Letter is a writer and visual artist living in South Florida, where she teaches literature and creative writing to undergraduates at Florida Atlantic University. Her writing has appeared or is forthcoming in *Louisiana Literature*, *storySouth*, *Fringe Magazine*, *Cutthroat*, *Aced Magazine*, *Specs*, and *Perigee*, among others. Learn more about Amy at http://amyletter.com.

GINA MARIE MAMMANO V.
A LENTEN MEDITATION
Poetry

Gina Marie Mammano V. is a poet, assemblage artist, teacher, alternative worship leader, and musician. She is passionate about communities gathering, entering into sacred spaces, and helping people find places of beauty and healing. She lives in San Juan Capistrano with her amazing husband and children, and loves to wander into the interiors of things.

AMANDA MCQUADE
GRACE
Poetry

Amanda McQuade studied American literature in Ohio. Her poetry and short fiction have recently appeared in *Mississippi Crow* and *Ruminate*. Currently, she writes and terrorizes the region of Charlotte, North Carolina.

DARREN J. N. MIDDLETON
JAPANESE PILGRIMAGE
SEXT, FEBRUARY 25, 2007
Poetry

A native of the U. K., Darren J. N. Middleton now serves as Associate Professor of Theology and Literature at Texas Christian University, which is located in Fort Worth, Texas. He has published six books, the most recent of which is *Theology after Reading: Christian Imagination and the Power of Fiction* (Baylor University Press, 2008). His poems have appeared in *Epworth Review*.

JAY RUBIN
FRUIT OF THE VINE
TUMORS
Poetry

Jay Rubin teaches writing at The College of Alameda in the San Francisco Bay Area and publishes *Alehouse*, an all-poetry literary journal. Check out the *Alehouse* website at www.alehousepress.com. He holds an MFA in Poetry from New England College and lives in San Francisco with his wife and son.

MARTHA SERPAS
EPITHALAMIA
NOW HILL
PARADIS
Poetry

Martha Serpas has published two collections of poetry, *Côte Blanche* (New Issues, 2002) and *The Dirty Side of the Storm* (Norton, 2006). Her work has appeared in *The New Yorker*, the *New York Times Book Review*, *The Christian Century*, and *Southwest Review*. She has taught at Yale Divinity School, the

University of Houston, and the University of Tampa, where she is currently an associate professor of English. She is poetry editor of *Tampa Review*.

BRIAN SPEARS
HALL RAISING
Editor's Choice in Poetry

Brian Spears is not related to the singer, but he does have a teenaged daughter named Brittany. He hopes she will forgive him one day. His work has appeared in many journals, including *The Southern Review*, *Louisiana Literature*, and *Measure*. He was a Stegner Fellow from 2003 - 2005 and currently teaches at Florida Atlantic University. He is the founder and chief blogger at Incertus (http://incertus.blogspot.com), and lives with the writer Amy Letter and their two cats, Wally and Eliot.

JENNIFER G. STEWART
ALL SAINTS' DAY, ISTANBUL
WALKING BACK TO THE FERRY, BÜYÜKADA
Poetry

Jennifer Stewart recently returned to northern Colorado after three years teaching composition and literature at LCC International University in the Baltic port town of Klaipeda, Lithuania. Before teaching in Lithuania, she earned degrees in rhetoric, composition and literature from Colorado State University and Bethel University in St. Paul, Minnesota. She has published previously in *Phantasmagoria*, and *The Priscilla Papers*. She loves words in all their forms, the Rocky Mountains, and Lithuanian Šaltibarščiai (cold beet soup).

JUNED SUBHAN
HIDING
Fiction

An English Literature graduate from Glasgow University, Juned Subhan has been published in numerous journals including *The Critical Quarterly*, *Ontario Review*, *North American Review*, *Cimarron Review*, *Indiana Review*, *Louisiana Literature*, *Marginalia*, *Bryant Literary Review*, *Descant*, *Westerly*, and *Southerly*. "Hiding" is taken from a complete collection titled, "Will You Remember Me?" He is currently working on his first novel.

LARRY D. THOMAS
DAFFODILS
HE CLOTHES THEM
IN SIN SO CRAFTILY MORTAL
Poetry

Larry Thomas is a "non-institutional" Christian, very tolerant of other religious persuasions, and has published nine collections of poems, most recently *New and Selected Poems* (TCU Press, 2008). His tenth poetry collection, *The Circus*, is forthcoming from Right Hand Pointing in 2009. For many years, he has been a regular contributor of poetry to *Windhover: A Journal of Christian Literature*, and a number of other national literary magazines. In April 2007, he was appointed by the Texas Legislature as the 2008 Texas Poet Laureate.

DON THOMPSON
PATER NOSTER
Poetry

Don Thompson and his wife live on her family cotton farm in the southern San Joaquin Valley, and their adopted Chinese baby girl just graduated from college. He has taught for many years at a nearby prison. A chapbook about the 60s, *Sittin' on Grace Slick's Stoop*, was published by Pudding house last year. *Turning Sixty* just came out from March Street Press, which published *Been There, Done That* a few years ago. Check them out, please. *Where We Live* is scheduled by Parallel Press (University of Wisconsin) for next spring.

SHANNA POWLUS WHEELER
WHISTLER
Poetry

Native to central Pennsylvania, Shanna Powlus Wheeler studied poetry at Penn State University, where she received her MFA in 2007. Poems from her first book manuscript, *Lo & Behold*, have appeared in *Crab Orchard Review*, *North American Review*, *The Evansville Review*, *The Christian Century*, *Christianity and Literature*, *Mezzo Cammin*, and other journals. Her book reviews have appeared in *The Missouri Review* and *The Southeast Review*. She directs the writing center and teaches composition at Lycoming College in Williamsport, Pennsylvania.

Announcing the Relief Writer's Database

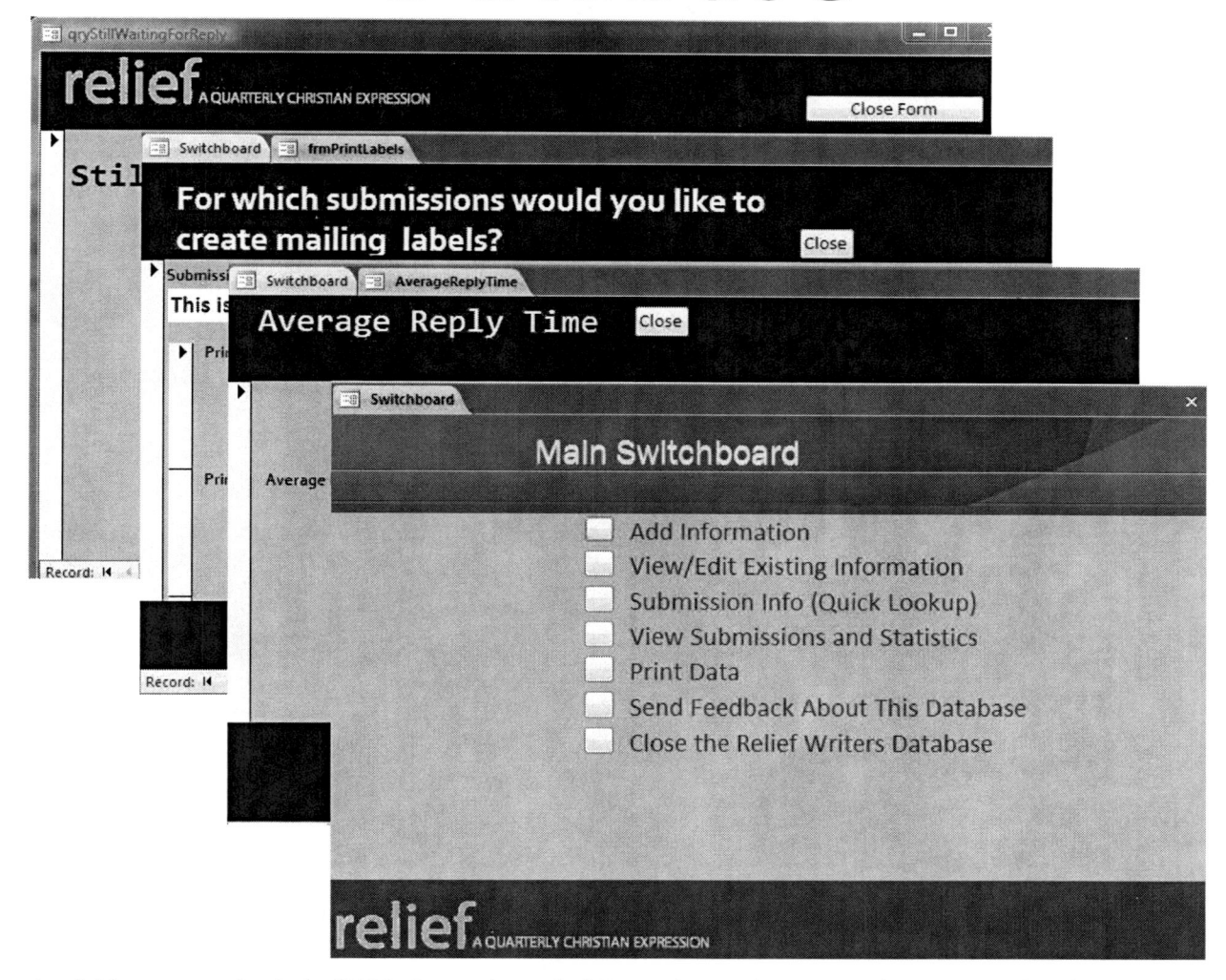

Available now on the Relief Web Store, the Relief Writer's Database is an electronic tool to help writers keep track of submissions, replies, and average journal response times. It even creates mailing labels, SASEs, and more! Designed by our very own Heather von Doehren, it saves time and is easy to use. Sorry Mac users, but at this time, the Relief Writer's Database is only for Windows XP and Vista.

Available only from the Relief Store! Click on the Purchase Button at ReliefJournal.com!

relief.
A QUARTERLY CHRISTIAN EXPRESSION

Volume 2
Issue 1

Mario Susko
Helen W. Mallon
Linda MacKillop
David Borofka
Rick Mullin
Allison Smythe
J. Stephen Rhodes
and more

CHRISTIAN WRITING

Continue your literary journey in 2008 with Fiction, Creative Nonfiction, and Poetry from the authors of *Relief: A Quarterly Christian Expression*. Decidedly not safe for the whole family, *Relief* is Christian writing without boundaries. Come visit us at http://www.reliefjournal.com!

UNBOUND

How do you exact revenge on a crotchety old neighbor without risking either jail time or a severe dent in your self esteem?

My Name Is Russell Fink

A Novel by Michael Snyder

"Snyder's writing is inventive and fun"
--Publishers Weekly

"Biting humor and an offbeat, dysfunctional protagonist shape this story of reconciliation"
--Library Journal

It comes out in March. Go buy it. Seriously, you'll like it. It's written by Michael Snyder, *Relief's* Editor's Choice winner from our very first issue. We like Mike. So will you.

Available from fine book sellers everywhere March 2008.

RUTGERS UNIVERSITY PRESS
Turning the Page in Publishing

Mama, PhD
Women Write about Motherhood and Academic Life
Edited by Elrena Evans and Caroline Grant $19.95 • 272 pages

Elrena Evans and Caroline Grant bring together thirty-five deeply felt personal narratives to explore the continued inequality of the sexes in higher education and suggest changes that could make universities more family-friendly workplaces. Candid, provocative and delivered, at times, with a wry sense of humor.

"All those sleepless nights and dirty diapers and baby food in your hair—where's the discursive construction of motherhood when you need it? It's here, in these smart, funny, poignant essays that struggle to balance mind and body, to balance body and soul."
—Catherine Newman, PhD, author of *Waiting for Birdy: A Year of Frantic Tedium, Neurotic Angst,* and *The Wild Magic of Growing a Family*

"A charming, heartfelt book that expresses the difficulties and the joys of combining a life in academia with motherhood. Each story is different, but the experiences and challenges are widely shared."
—Mary Ann Mason, author of *Mothers on the Fast Track: How a New Generation Can Balance Families and Careers*

Visit http://www.mamaphd.com/ and http://www.elrenaevans.com to view the author trailer and read an excerpt!

***Relief* readers can receive a 20% discount and free shipping by using the following code: 02MAMA08 on our website or by calling 800-848-6224**

RUTGERS UNIVERSITY PRESS
rutgerspress.rutgers.edu
Available wherever books are sold
For alerts and discounts, subscribe to RU Reading?
Rutgers, The State University of New Jersey

COACH'S MIDNIGHT DINER

SECOND EDITION

COMING OCTOBER 2008

COACH'S MIDNIGHT DINER

A HARDBOILED GENRE ANTHOLOGY OF HORROR, MYSTERY, ADVENTURE, PARANORMAL, AND WEIRD FICTION WITH A CHRISTIAN SLANT

THE JESUS VS. CTHULHU EDITION IS NOW ON SALE AT BARNESANDNOBLE.COM

SUBMISSIONS FOR THE SECOND EDITION ARE NOW CLOSED

THE SECOND EDITION WILL BE SHIPPING IN OCTOBER 2008

WARNING: THE INTENSITY LEVEL HAS BEEN RAISED READ AT YOUR OWN RISK

VISIT THE NEW WEBSITE AT
WWW.THEMIDNIGHTDINER.COM

The following bonus story is a preview of the upcoming second edition of *Coach's Midnight Diner*, a genre anthology of horror, mystery, crime, and paranormal fiction. I sneak one in at the end of every issue of *Relief*. "The Denial" is an interesting piece that speculates on two natures, one human, one not so much. Enjoy!

~Coach Culbertson, Proprietor

THE DENIAL
Maggie Stiefvater

You can't deny your nature, that's what they all said. But they were wrong. The moment that I wanted Lily Gable, wanted her like wanting to be with her instead of wanting to be *in* her, I had denied my nature.

She was an interesting girl, Lily, which I suppose is how it happened. The denying my nature and becoming one of one, instead one of many, I mean. She lived in an apartment just off campus, by herself. Well, she had a hamster, as well—damn ugly thing it was too, because someone had thrown hot oil at it before Lily took it on. Anyway, aside from the fugly hamster, she lived alone, and she was putting herself through college writing bumper sticker and t-shirt slogans and selling them online.

I remember the first time Lily made me laugh, watching her outside her window on a dull, rainy night. She was sitting on her bed, her laptop on the vintage quilt, knees folded up on either side of her face like a grasshopper, and she was thinking about her unpaid electric bill. There weren't any lights on in the room, other than her laptop, because she wanted to save energy.

This was a waste of effort, by the way, because it was actually a miscalculation on the part of the power company, but she didn't know that. I thought about making it right, fixing the problem and erasing the frown-lines from over her fine light eyebrows. I think that was the beginning for me.

Anyway, she was trying to write a bumper sticker that would sell well enough to pay the bogus electric bill, and finally she swore and typed Honk if you're hotter than me.

And I laughed.

Then I became human.

No, that's not true, really. Wipe that from the record. I wasn't quite human. But I was a hell of a lot closer than I had been before.

God, that's funny. Hell of a lot closer. Sorry, I amuse myself.

So of course I wanted to get closer to her. I was too chicken-shit to actually talk to her at first, so I followed her. I waited outside in the shadows, watching her come home from her classes, shoulders bundled up against the cold, backpack covered with beaded rain from the walk. And

I was there in the morning too, an anonymous figure on a bench, one of hundreds she passed every day. As she walked by me, I could see her peering at the cars that went by, reading the bumper stickers. Every so often her lips would move, and I would know that she was trying one out.

Everything in life was funny to Lily. She always had a grin on her face. Not a Pollyanna sort of grin. What, did you think I would do this to myself for a nice Pollyanna girl? No, she laughed at things like people on painfully obvious first dates—the ones that weren't going well. She grinned at middle-aged women scrubbing the alloy wheels of their husbands' BMWs on the curb as they parallel parked. She smirked when high-powered businessmen stepped in melted ice cream on the sidewalk and tracked it into their offices.

I loved it when she smirked. Her eyebrows got all pointy and her mouth got small. Like she was blowing out birthday candles.

Anyway. It took me a long time to actually follow her from her apartment, and the day I chose to follow her, it turned out she was going to church. Well, spank my ass and call me Jesus. I hadn't ever thought of her as a church-going type, probably because one of her best-selling stickers was In Case of the Rapture, Can I Have Your Big-Screen? But there she was, in a skirt that was probably a bit too short to really be chaste, heading into St. Michael the Archangel's on Grass Street, not at all awkward.

I followed her in. It was weird to enter a church under my own steam, instead of riding on someone's shoulders. Inside St. Michael's, it was dim and too-warm, smelling of many bodies, some of which were wearing adult diapers. Lily took a seat up front, and I took a cautious seat on the edge of a pew, waiting to burst into flame or become a pillar of salt or some other crap that ought to happen to me in a church.

"Mommy," a voice whispered beside me.

"Shhh."

"That man's not a Christian."

I looked to see who was talking. It was a little blonde boy. I'm bad at ages, but he was old enough to not smell like the people wearing adult diapers but not old enough to drive or swear.

"Shhh," his mother whispered in his ear. "People with tattoos can be Christians too."

I had tattoos? I hadn't realized. Oh, shit, yeah. Look, there was one on my arm, a dragon eating its own tail or something. That was wicked cool.

The little boy leaned towards me. "Do you believe in God?"

"Hell, yeah," I told him. Far more than he did.

The mother gave me a hard look; I looked back with half a smile. She was hot, and the deep V-neck of her top showed me the edges of her breasts. I finished my smile so she'd know that I noticed. She slid a little further down the pew.

In front, Lily stood when everyone else stood and kneeled when everyone else knelt. Her lips moved the same way everyone else's did. Damn. Of course she was Catholic. Whatever. I could handle that.

But after learning of her mad skillz with holy water, it took weeks for me to approach her again. Weeks during which I learned about hunger and work. My tattoos hadn't come with a trade, so I fell back into old habits to make money: deceiving people. It was not quite giving into my nature as I deceived for entertainment rather than for the pleasure of it.

And so when I finally showed myself to her, I was not a nobody. I was not a somebody yet either, but I had a name: Nick Bishop, and some people knew it.

Lily came down the stairs of her apartment, backpack slung over her shoulder, and she paused when she saw me standing on the sidewalk at the base of them. Her eyes lifted up and down me and for a moment I wondered what my shaved head, my black eyes, my black coat would get, if they would get a grin, or a laugh, or a smirk. They got none of those. Instead, her eyes narrowed, studying me as I stood there, a black blot on the white sidewalk.

I spread my arms out and then brought them over my head, fingers reaching towards the sky as if I could claw heaven down. Doves burst from my sleeves, wings beating against my fingers in their struggle to vanish up into the steel gray morning.

Lily's mouth pulled up on one side and she made a grudging noise of approval. Her eyes finally dropped from my face to my feet, where there were some coins and bills from the tricks I had done while waiting for her. Stepping to the bottom of the stairs, she began to rummage in her pockets for change.

I smiled at her. Friendly but approachable, not too much teeth. I wanted to befriend her, not eat her. See—denying my nature. "Just your attention is enough. May I have it?"

She raised an eyebrow. It was pointy. "You have it."

"Besides," I added, wanting to turn the one pointy eyebrow into two pointy ones, "You already gave me something."

I opened my hand and showed her a delicate gold cross on a chain. Her hand went to her neck, pulling down her turtleneck. Goosebumps raised immediately as her bare skin touched the frigid air.

She made a face, though she didn't reward me with a full smirk.

"But—" I took her hand, touching her for the first time in a millennia, and cupped the cross back into her palm. Her eyes were on the back of my hand, on the blue and green star tattoos that disappeared into my sleeve. "I already told you I only wanted your attention. So thanks. But no thanks."

She smirked, now that she had her cross again. "You're good."

I grinned.

Lily went to class. After she had gone, I stayed on the sidewalk in front of her apartment for a long time, imagining being invited in, sitting on her bed and watching over her shoulder as she typed bumper stickers.

While I loitered, a few passersby eyed me, and I did some tricks for them. One of them was a little boy with a yellow puppy on a leash. In the old days, I would've turned his puppy's skin inside-out to make the boy cry and then would've slid away into the cracks of the sidewalk like beads of mercury. Instead, I made dog biscuits appear in my cold-numbed hands and underneath his father's ridiculous hat. The father gave me a twenty and led the boy and the dog away.

The weeks went by, and each day, when Lily came out of her apartment, I was waiting. One day, I turned pebbles into rosebuds. Another day, I levitated her backpack and made her pass her hand underneath so that she could see that it really floated. The next week, I made a puddle of water appear on the sidewalk at her feet, and spat a small boat into it. Both vanished when she stepped into the water, grinning.

"You're good," she said, and went to class.

One frozen day, when she came out of her apartment, days before her winter vacation, I clouded the icy air with my breath until the mist birthed a butterfly.

Lily made a soft noise and clapped her hands around the insect, making a cage for it with her palms. "Asshole," she said, but her voice was fond. "It'll die. It is real, isn't it?"

I hadn't thought of its fate but I supposed it would freeze in this D.C. winter. It didn't seem that important. Butterflies died all the time. "Real as you."

"I have to bring it inside. Unless you can magic it someplace warm."

But she was already half-turned towards the door as I shrugged. She looked over her shoulder. "Will you freeze as well, in this weather?"

I tilted my chin up, held out my arms in my long black coat, a giant dark bird. "Anything's possible."

"Come inside and have some coffee."

I gestured down the sidewalk. "Don't you have to hurry—hurry to your classes like always?"

"I have made them magically disappear," Lily said. "Like you would. Get the door for me."

So we went inside the studio apartment that I had watched for so many months, where I had first heard her laugh at her own jokes, all alone in her room, with only my invisible presence as company. It was brighter than I remembered, the light all white and blue from the icy white sky out the windows. There was her laptop, sitting on the faded plaid couch, a bumper sticker stuck on the back of it. I turned my head to read it: Veterinarians Do It Doggy-Style.

Lily walked into the center of the living room, the light from the tall windows illuminating her slender form as she uncupped her hands.

The butterfly lay still in her palms and she moaned. "Oh, dammit. I think I've killed it."

I walked over and looked into her hands. She hadn't killed it, but it had fluttered against her hands so hard in its fear that its wings were ruined. Worse than dead, it had been drawn down from a creature of the air to no better than a roach or ant. I looked up at her eyebrows, drawn down low over her coffee-colored eyes, and at the line of sad frustration that her mouth made.

"Silly girl," I told her, and laid my hands over the top of her palms. Beneath my fingers, I felt the butterfly's lace wings kiss my skin, moving faster and faster. I lifted my hand from hers and the butterfly flew into the air, a small patch of her quilt rising over our heads and dancing in the light of the window.

Lily's eyebrows drew together for a second as she watched it fly through her apartment, as out of place as I was, and I thought that she would call me out, tell me that what I had done was real magic, not sleight of hand. But then her fleeting frown became her easy grin as she fell into the willing suspension of disbelief that all magicians relied on. I wouldn't have to lie to her about the ridiculous kindness I'd done for her, though lying was something I was even better at.

"I'll leave the magic to you." Lily went on the other side of the counter to make coffee, and I sat on a stool on my side. "Milk? Sugar?"

"Black," I said truthfully.

"Hope this isn't too strong," she said, and slid a mug over. She leaned against the counter towards me, boobs pushed together, but I was looking at her hands, imagining her reaching out to take mine. Imagining what it would feel like, touching my cheek softly just before she went to sleep. "So. Nick Bishop." She said it as if she was trying the words out in her head, like I had when I'd decided on the name in the first place. "That's a name everyone's saying these days."

"Is it."

Lily held up her mug to her lips without drinking it. "They say that you're going to be the greatest magician of our generation."

I grinned at her. "Who's they?"

"People."

"People who know what they're talking about?"

Lily smirked. "Not generally. But a lot of people are saying it anyway. They say you came out of nowhere."

"Nothing comes from nowhere," I said. I drank the coffee. It was too strong. It tasted like battery acid.

"So where did you come from, Nick Bishop the magician?"

She didn't mean it seriously, but I answered that way. "Hell." No one could say I had lied to her. No one could say I denied what I was.

"Wow, it must've been pretty bad if D.C. was a step up," Lily laughed. "Remind me not to visit."

"Don't visit." The idea of her there, the demons scratching their nails on her flesh, pulling her mouth into a scream, was so physically painful that I shuddered, bile in my throat. The memory of my nails in flesh, my teeth ripping hair—

"Coffee's that bad?"

I looked at her and for a moment I couldn't remember what language she was speaking. Then I laughed. "Like oil. Like dirty oil."

"Sorry. Want a fresh cup? I can try again. Second time's the charm."

Friggin' get it together. I smiled, no teeth at all. "No, thanks, I could use the protein."

Lily smiled at me. "I like you, Nick Bishop the magician."

The winter passed us by, Lily and I. Her butterfly did not die and neither did she. Soon I couldn't wait outside her apartment for her, because the crowds to see me were too large. So Lily told me to stay in her apartment, and I did, sleeping on her couch, and doing magic for ever larger audiences who brought their willing suspension of disbelief in their pockets and purses. I had earned enough money to move out, but I didn't. I had earned enough of Lily's desire to move into her bedroom, but I didn't.

I made doves appear on stage, pouring out of vases of flowers that had been nothing but coat hangers a moment before. I poured rainbows from my hands and pulled keys from my mouth; rainbows from far-away rains and keys to doors that would never open again. And the crowds shouted that they loved me, and that I was God, and I denied that I loved it, that I loved being lifted above everyone else and wielding power far beyond them.

I denied, too, that I brought darkness to Lily's apartment. I denied that the shadows were deeper in her living room than they had been that winter, that her eyes were dimmer, that I was slipping from one of one, to one of many again, and that the many were hungry.

By next autumn, Lily's grins were gone, so too her smirks. Her laughs hurt my ears, because they denied her nature.

I returned to the apartment one night after a show and found it dark. So dark that even I could not see through the blackness of the night. The light over the oven was on, but it seemed dim and faraway, like a ship bobbing distantly on an ocean.

"Lily?" I called, and the darkness ate my voice.

I moved through the kitchen, found the couch, saw that it was unoccupied, and moved towards the bedroom door. I had never been inside. I could not allow myself to want her, because what else would I want?

But behind the door, I heard water running, and that seemed wrong. I didn't waste my breath saying her name again. I just pushed through the door, into the drowning darkness of the bedroom.

It was ten thousand times worse in this room than it had been in the darkest of the shadows of the living room, and now I heard the silent voices laughing at me. Laughing that I shouldn't have thought that I was an individual, that I shouldn't have singled out a human for my peculiar brand of love. I'd never thought that they would've emerged for the unique pleasure of tormenting one of their own by tormenting her.

I burst into the bathroom, and found Lily laying in the bathtub in a tank-top and jeans. The water covered the tiles, the soles of my shoes, her mouth. Her hair floated out around her.

"Lily," I said again. I didn't know if she'd magically made herself disappear, like her classes, if she was dead in my hands like a butterfly, or if she had merely beaten her wings useless in her fear. I reached into the water, lifted her from the tub, and lay her across my lap.

Movement in the tub caught my eye, and I saw the butterfly—our butterfly—floating slowly by on the surface of the water, dead. She'd drowned it.

"Fuck, Lily," I said, clutching her to me. I wanted her. I wanted her to be mine. I wanted her to hold my hand, damn it, I wanted her to love me. I wanted her alive. I wanted her to touch my face.

Her eyebrows were damp and sad, so far away from the smirk that I had loved that it was hard to imagine it was the same girl. She was supposed to have made me happy.

I bent my head and touched her forehead with mine, her nose against my nose, so close that my lips almost were touching hers, mine hot, hers cold. The darkness pushed in against the florescent bathroom lights, urging me to take her if I wanted her, to destroy her and take her into myself. To throw off this human form I'd taken, to bear her soul back home with me, to make her touch me and force her brows into the smirk I liked.

But.

I can deny my nature.

The voices laughed wildly, too many and too varied to count.

I put my hand on Lily's face, on her cheek, and then I kissed her, like I had wanted to for months.

Suck her out, the darkness said. Take it out.

I pulled my lips away from hers. "Lily," I said, "I think I want you to be happy."

The darkness was silent.

Lily took a breath. I carried her back into her bedroom, and I turned on the lights. They pushed back the shadows, but not completely. I was one of many. I laid Lily on the bed and watched her pulse in her neck for a moment. Then I went back into the bathroom and scooped the limp butterfly out of the tub.

When I went back into the bedroom and opened the window to the night, her eyes opened. "Nick. Nick."

"Lily, I love you," I said. I laid my hand over the top of the butterfly, waited until I could feel the soft fluttering of wings against my fingers, and then I opened my hands.

Lily propped her body up and watched my stolen body fall to the ground. I lifted up into the air, my lacy wings fluttering in the light breeze, and I flew out the window, dragging the shadows behind me.

And she began to laugh, tears running down her face.

MAGGIE STIEFVATER is a 26-year-old full time author who lives in Virginia with her husband, two small children, and two dogs who fart a lot. She used to play bagpipes competitively and now plays harp, tin whistle, piano, and guitar whenever she can get her hands on them. Her debut novel for young adults, *Lament*, features homicidal faeries and will be hitting bookstores in October 2008.

Printed in the United States
204313BV00004B/105-184/P